SIEGFRIED SASSOON
LETTERS TO MAX BEERBOHM
with a few answers

Mr. Siegfried Sassoon

mx
1931

Siegfried Sassoon
Letters to Max Beerbohm
with a few answers

edited by
Rupert Hart-Davis

faber and faber
LONDON · BOSTON

First published in 1986 by
Faber and Faber Limited
3 Queen Square London WC1N 3AU

Printed in Great Britain by
Butler & Tanner Ltd, Frome, Somerset

British Library Cataloguing in Publication Data

Sassoon, Siegfried
Letters to Max Beerbohm
1. Sassoon, Siegfried——Biography 2. Poets,
English——20th century——Biography
I. Title II. Hart-Davis, Rupert
821'.912 PR6037.A86Z/

ISBN 0-571-13899-3.

Library of Congress Cataloging-in-Publication Data

· Sassoon, Siegfried
Letters to Max Beerbohm
1. Sassoon, Siegfried, 1886–1967——Correspondence.
2. Beerbohm, Max, Sir, 1872–1956——Correspondence.
3. Authors, English——20th century——Correspondence.
I. Beerbohm, Max, Sir, 1872–1956. II. Sassoon, Siegfried,
1886–1967. III. Hart-Davis, Rupert, 1907– .
PR6037.A86Z483 1986 821'.912 86–11552
ISBN 0-571-13899-3

Introduction

This book is to celebrate the centenary of Siegfried Sassoon's birth on 8 September 1886. I am sure that, rather than a critical study of his work, or even a further volume of his diaries (which will follow later), he would prefer this happy tribute to one of his most admired and dearly loved friends. Max Beerbohm hated writing letters, so the paucity of his answers is not surprising, but luckily Siegfried's diaries fill in many gaps.

Max was fourteen years older than Siegfried and had lived in London until 1910, when he relinquished his post as dramatic critic of the *Saturday Review*, married the American actress Florence Kahn, who was four years his junior, and went to live in the Villino Chiaro outside Rapallo, on the coast between Genoa and La Spezia. He spent the rest of his life there, except for brief visits to London for exhibitions of his caricatures, and the years of the two wars.

All ten Max letters are in the Humanities Research Center at Austin, Texas, as are eighteen of Siegfried's and the manuscript of his diary-record of his 1937 visit to Rapallo. Twenty-nine Siegfried letters are in the Max Room at Merton College, Oxford, and five belong to Max's sister-in-law Mrs Eva Reichmann.

I am grateful to Lord Astor of Hever for permission to print a letter from his grandfather. For help with footnote research and other kindnesses I am much indebted to the Marquess of Anglesey, John Burgass of Merton College, Paul Chipchase, Janet Green, Cathy Henderson of the Humanities Research Center, Ernest and Joyce Mehew, Charles Moore, Richard Ormond, James Smeall, and Oliver Stonor.

Marske-in-Swaledale   RUPERT HART-DAVIS
June 1986

Siegfried Sassoon and Max Beerbohm first met at the London home of the critic and autobiographer Edmund Gosse in the late summer of 1916, when Max and Florence were living in England because of the war, and Siegfried was on convalescent leave from the army.

On 6 June 1922 Siegfried dined with Gosse, and

As usual, we performed a rite of unstinted eulogy at the shrine of Max Beerbohm: 'The one indisputably exquisite prose-writer of our age.' For Max's art is the quintessence of Gosse's appreciation of life.

The second meeting, again at the Gosses', was on 21 May 1923.

Max was not talkative, but quite charming. I shared a taxi back to Jermyn Street with them (they are staying with the William Nicholsons).[1] When saying goodnight, I felt impelled to say, with a bashful air, 'I think you are one of the best authors.' 'How delightful of you,' was the appropriate reply, and it was duly forthcoming. (My remark was gospel truth.)

Siegfried read everything that Max published, visited all his exhibitions at the Leicester Galleries, and bought eight of his caricatures. He sent his privately printed volumes of verse to Max, who, always an unwilling correspondent, seldom even acknowledged their receipt. Their next meeting is recorded in Siegfried's diary:

31 December 1928
Went to 11 Apple Tree Yard[2] at three o'clock, to talk to Nicholson about his illustrations for *Memoirs*.[3] We sat for an

---

[1] W.N., painter (1872–1949), knighted 1936, and his second wife Edie, *née* Phillips (1890–1958).

[2] In a cul-de-sac between Jermyn Street and St James's Square, where William Nicholson had a studio-cottage.

[3] The illustrated edition of S.S.'s *Memoirs of a Fox-Hunting Man* (1928) appeared in 1929.

hour in the little parlour downstairs. He did sketches and then we talked about Robert Graves, Nancy and Laura.[1] W.N. agrees with me that R.G. is rather impossible now. W.N. also mentioned Max being in London, and I thought how nice it would be to see him. N. took me upstairs to show me his picture of Beatrice and Sidney Webb. And there was Max, quietly sitting at a little writing-table by the door. I hadn't seen him for about four years. Florence Beerbohm came in later. And then Florence Hardy![2] Also a Mr Harrison (a bearded painter), smart and elderly, and agreeable.[3]

Max had been lunching with old Lady Lewis,[4] who had fainted at the table (she is eighty-three). W.N. left at 5.30 to catch a train, but I stayed there till 7. Max stimulated me, and I actually made an impromptu which seemed to please him. I said of Osbert Sitwell 'Everything that he touches turns to publicity.' Before Mrs B. and the others arrived, and while N. was absent on some errand, I had a talk with Max, mostly about Gosse and Hardy (and the funeral etc of T.H.). Later on Max said 'Supposing that the Great Sentimentalist (Barrie) were to leave instructions that his heart was to be buried at 23 Campden Hill Square.[5] The autopsy takes place, but the doctors find that – there is no heart!' It was said in that deprecating voice which can't be reproduced. Also the slight shrug and deprecating manner and look.

I longed to be alone with him. His wife is not interesting, and is by no means self-effacing. They are coming to tea here next week! What luck!

9 January 1929
Another dark day; foggy. Max Beerbohm and his wife arrived at 4.50. Max wearing a heavy sealskin-lined coat.

---

[1] Nicholson's daughter Nancy was married to Graves. Laura Riding was his mistress.
[2] Widow of Thomas Hardy.
[3] Lawrence Alexander (Peter) Harrison, portrait-painter (1867–1937). He was married to the soprano Alma Strettel, and they were both close friends of the American artist J.S. Sargent (1856–1925).
[4] Widow of Sir George Lewis, the most successful solicitor of his time.
[5] Where J.M. Barrie had lived before S.S. rented a flat there.

He was pleased when he saw my eight drawings from his exhibition. We were looking at them (after I'd made the tea) when Stephen[1] arrived. Max talked about John Davidson,[2] Count Berchtold[3] and others in the drawings – in his slow finished way – like his prose. He also described Sir E. Sassoon[4] at 25 Park Lane. It was all delightful, and Stephen was happy. Max never sat down all the time, but strolled about the room smoking cigarettes and talking. They stayed one and a half hours.

On 23 November 1929 Siegfried and Stephen Tennant arrived at the Excelsior Hotel, Rapallo, on their way to Sicily. Next day they were at the Villino Chiaro from 12.30 till 6.15 and Siegfried recorded in his diary:

An enchanting experience, of which one can only say that it is as enjoyable as reading his books and looking at his drawings.

And again, after another visit two days later:

Ought I to write a detailed account of conversations with Max? I am disinclined. His style is so complete and so exquisitely entertaining. His leisurely anecdotes are so interwoven with his delicious little mimicries and social intonations. The hospitality of Mrs Max so perfect. Their liking for me and Stephen so blissfully comforting. Much wisdom underlies Max's humour and delicate raillery and exact observation of persons and things (mostly persons). To-day it was raining and blowing; the curtains were drawn at lunch, and we sat around the table by soft electric light, in a homely little universe of our own. Conversation was less of a *tour de force* than on Sunday. Max produces a feeling of having had just enough good wine to make one happy.

On 28 November:

To-day was wet, but that only made our cosy six hours (1–7)

---

[1] Siegfried's friend the Hon. Stephen Tennant (born 1906), son of the first Lord Glenconner.
[2] Scottish poet (1857–1909).
[3] Count Leopold von Berchtold, Austrian statesman (1863–1942).
[4] Sir Edward Sassoon (1856–1912), father of Sir Philip and a remote cousin of S.S.

at the Beerbohms' all the better. Max (wearing his almost-white tweed suit) was pink-faced and mellifluous as ever, discoursing to my delighted ears or listening with stimulating attentiveness to my own discursions. Mrs Max (in black) conversing freely with Stephen who has won her heart entirely. But what did we talk about, you ask. Can one condense six hours' incessant talk at the Maxes'? I can only hope that passages of the talk will revisit me in after years. 'I remember Max telling me when I saw him in 1929 ... etc.' Anyhow he has embellished my copy of *The Testament of Beauty* with a drawing of George V and a letter from George V to Dr Bridges.[1]

During the last hour he showed us an old photograph album (given him by Gordon Craig[2]) which had been made by Augustus Hare.[3] And the faded 1870 photos, of well-known and well-connected people, led him on to regret that he himself wasn't born in 1820 and died in 1887. 'If I'd been my present age in 1860, I should have been a crusted fogey,' he said. 'My temperament makes me dislike all innovations.' He was lamenting (at lunch also) the destruction of London – 'ferro-concrete rising up everywhere' – 'the Duke of Norfolk selling Norfolk House'. He spoke almost bitterly – almost petulantly – comparing London with the French, who have respected Paris since Baron Haussmann rebuilt much of it for them. Park Lane is already ruined – in three years the Adelphi will be gone, under the Charing Cross Scheme, and now even St James's Square!, adding 'But I don't care. If the English are such Philistines as to be indifferent to the destruction of their beautiful buildings, they deserve all that they get. A few letters to *The Times*, protesting against the latest outrage – that is the only outward sign of our dissatisfaction!'

---

[1] Robert Bridges's long poem (1929) bore an elaborate dedication to King George V in Gothic type. In the bottom corner of the page Max drew the King in naval uniform, pointing to the dedication and saying 'Wot, me?' The back endpapers contain an imaginary letter to the poet in the King's undistinguished hand.
[2] Actor, writer and stage-designer (1872–1966). Son of Ellen Terry.
[3] Autobiographer and topographical writer (1834–1903).

6

The poet W.B. Yeats and his wife were living in Rapallo, and after Siegfried had visited them 'Max wanted to hear all about our visit'.

I said I feared Yeats *was* a bit of a *poseur* ... Max said that the brilliant Irishmen in London had often been *poseurs*, but had helped to keep London alive and amused – from Goldsmith, Sheridan, Burke, Tom Moore, on to Wilde, George Moore, and Bernard Shaw. 'In the early Nineties conversation at lunches and dinners was mostly about Wilde. Between 1905 and 1910 everyone was talking of Moore and what he had said (and written). And Shaw was always being talked about since 1900 – some of Shaw's best work is in his letters.'

Max spoke of George Moore with intense dislike. Of Norman Douglas: 'There is a touch of the "codger" about him.' Of Galsworthy: 'He does the old uncles beautifully, but goes to pieces when describing "the way of a man with a maid" – nothing but moons (new, gibbous, and full), roses etc.' Of H.G. Wells: 'His novels are like collapsed blanc-manges, but always contain enjoyable passages.'

6 February 1930   *The Times*

Dear Mr Sassoon, There is to be an Imperial Press Conference in London next June when the Press of the United Kingdom will have as their guests some one-hundred *Delegates from all parts of the Empire, and their wives.* We will try to show them as much of England as possible in the month; and on the 16th June we are giving a Dinner at the Royal Academy, over which the *President* of the Royal Academy will *preside*, and at which we hope our guests will have an opportunity of meeting *representatives* of art and literature, and indeed of all the *professions.* A function of this kind during the season is *unprecedented* and we are very anxious that the gathering should be a *representative* one. On behalf of the Empire Press Union I very much hope we may have the pleasure of your company on this occasion. You will receive a card of invitation in due course. Yours sincerely   J.J. Astor[1]

---

[1] Colonel John Jacob Astor (1886–1971). Chief Proprietor of *The Times* 1922–66. Created Baron Astor of Hever 1956.

P.S. Can't you persuade your pal Beerbohm to come along? J.J.A.

Do I misread? . . . Quite credible, indeed, That at the belov'd
                                          R.A. the Press (U.K.)
Will 'dine' (as Rudyard K. might – roughly – say) 'Grub
                  Street from Martinique to Mandalay'.
Oh yes, they'll all agree 'Join hanns cross Shea'. But . . . can
                  such men make mincemeat of their *wives?*
The choice, from better half's anatomy (even for the Mother-
land's sake) of . . . what? . . . must be the Delegatest problem
                                          of their lives![1]

St Valentine's Day 1930   *Grand Hotel,*
                                  Villa Politi ai Cappuccini,
                                            Siracusa, Sicilia

Dear Max, I hope this will make you smile. One or two footnotes
seem to me essential owing to the unavoidable obscurity of the
poem.

(a) *'Join hanns cross Shea'* This is an attempt at 'liquid
    synaloepha'.[2] I hope you will consider that it 'sharpens the
    rhetoric and liberates the syntax' (*vide*: you know what).

(b) I was beginning to hope that there was, in modern life, less
    confusion between 'mincemeat' and 'helpmeet'. But it seems
    that I erred.

(c) Should I query this cannibalism before sending my final
    decision re acceptance? . . . 'All right, you needn't be rude; I
    only Astor question!' is how it might end?   Yours S.S.

Copy of Valentine sent to 'A.B.'[3]
Tootle-oo to All That

The panegyrics of the Press have smitten
One Fusilier to remonstration ribald . . .
Bennett: *'Good-Bye* is excellently written.'
Sassoon: *'All That* is excellently scribbled.'

---

[1] These lines are written between the first five lines of the above letter. The italics
and P.S. are by S.S.

[2] The contraction of two syllables into one.

[3] *Goodbye to All That* by Robert Graves (1929) had been warmly praised by
Arnold Bennett in the *Evening Standard*.

We like this place very much, and are staying till the end of the month. Stephen finds *marvellous* shells on the sea-shore, and is enraptured by them. I am still writing my book,[1] 'in doubt and great perplexity' (Tennyson).[2]

Siegfried's 1930 Diary

Rapallo 8 April

This afternoon I spent seventy-five minutes at Villino Chiaro. Talking to the Maxes, I realised that I am quite rusty as a talker, after conversing with no one but Stephen since December 2nd! But I was as garrulous as ever, and felt that there were endless things to talk about, and Max contributed his usual leisurely delights of commentary and invention, and the sun was shining as it never shone when we were here four months ago. Rapallo is a peaceful, welcoming place. I told Max all about how I managed to finish my book, and was told about Mrs Hardy's successful first visit to Italy. They call her 'The Debutante' because she was so young and happy! And we discussed *Her Privates We* (which I finished before lunch). Max knows the author,[3] and lent me his *Scenes and Portraits*.

10 April

What a luxury it is to listen to Max! He gives one his very best all the time, as he does in his writings and drawings. To me he is the ideal wit and critic combined. Elegant and fastidious and retrospective as he is, his standards are vigorous and stimulating. Tolerant and urbane and withdrawn from the 'big noise' of modernity, he still seems to be keeping a critical eye on everything worth noticing.

Yesterday he expressed a sort of antipathy to certain things – T.S. Eliot ('a case of the Emperor wearing no clothes') and D.H. Lawrence ('a diseased mind'). Not altogether in favour of E.M.

---

[1] *Memoirs of an Infantry Officer*, published 18 September 1930.
[2] 'The Palace of Art', line 278.
[3] Frederic Manning, poet and essayist (1887–1935). His *Scenes and Portraits* was first published in 1909, *Her Privates We* in 1930.

Forster either, admitting that he'd not been able to get beyond Chapter One of *A Passage to India*, and had disagreed with certain points of view in *Aspects of the Novel*. Has only read one Lawrence novel, *Women in Love* – one of the worst – much of which Max calls 'balderdash'; 'a clumsy writer', he says. He'd been antagonized by Lawrence's preface to Magnus's *Foreign Legion* – one of his unworthiest efforts.[1] I suggested that some of the short stories are very fine. But how *could* Max hit it off with Lawrence? (a tough proposition for most of us! – though he is at present Stephen's greatest idol). Eliot he called 'a dried bean' (I agree with that!) and compared him with Browning, 'gigantic and fertile continent of creative resourcefulness compared with the melancholy back-yard of Tom Eliot, who sits there ironically analysing an empty sardine-tin'. Browning led him to give me a beautiful précis of Henry James's short story about Browning and Leighton (which I must read).[2] Browning's unpopularity in society, and the difficulty of reconciling his loud underbred outward self with the poet who wrote so finely. The background at Villino Chiaro is so engaging and endearing. Yesterday there was much concern about a newly-arrived pair of white pigeons.

Max and I pacing sedately up and down – now and then going into the little square room with its indigo blue walls – I got him on to Whistler (J.M. – not Rex, though Rex is a favourite of his) and he took out the copy of *The Gentle Art* which is the subject of one of his best essays.[3] Conversing with Max, everything turns to entertainment and delectable humour and evocation of the past. Of de la Mare – I dropped in a reference to his questioning habit of mind – Max said 'Yes, I'm too young to be able to remember Socrates, so de la Mare is the most *questioning* man I've ever met!' (and of course we agreed that he is one of the most delightful of men). Not a thousandth part can be recorded. But I feel that these talks with Max permanently enrich my mind, and no doubt much

---

[1] *Memoirs of the Foreign Legion* by M.M. with an [83-page] introduction by D.H. Lawrence (1924).

[2] 'The Private Life' in James's volume of that name (1893).

[3] *The Gentle Art of Making Enemies* (1890). Max's essay 'Whistler's Writing' appeared in *Yet Again* (1909). For Rex see p. 70.

of it will recur spontaneously in future memories; he is like travelling abroad – one feels the benefit afterwards.

Some day I shall want to recreate my conversations with him. *I must try and 'learn him by heart'*. But after six hours' talk I am glutted with the delicate fare with which he has loaded me, and can only say 'Thank you, Max, a thousand times, for restoring my faith in delicacy, and perfection of manners, mental and hospitable, in the graces of life and philosophy.' He has just heard from Edinburgh University that they propose to confer an Honorary Degree on him. This evidently pleases him (as it does me, if it causes him to visit England this summer) though he was wondering what Sir Otto Beit has done to earn an Hon.Ll.D.[1] – Sir Otto being one of this procession, which also includes J.J. Jusserand.[2]

11 April

Max gladdened me by demolishing Wyndham Lewis, as a writer. I am so tired of being told that Lewis is a great prose genius, and have always suspected him of being a very confused and inexpert technician. Most of our talk was delectable gossip – occasionally I was reminded of my talks with Gosse – the texture of our talk had the same quality, except that Max is never malicious, though Gosse's maliciousness was always entertaining. The similarity, I think, is in the quality of a certain *reticence*, and a sort of convention of *polite* exchange of ideas and personalities – no clumsy blurtings and indiscretions – and an elegance of expression in which Max's 'social form' (as he calls it) resembles Gosse's. And of course – being a bit of a chameleon – I adapt my style to his, and talk more elaborately (less tersely) than I would do with a less accomplished talker than Max (who probably finds me a bit long-winded at times!). But how I love leisurely talk – especially on that roof – with the blue expanse of sea beyond the parapet-wall creating an illusion of our being suspended in the sky – high above the world – and on the other side the charming little garden, and beyond the garden-wall the steep hill with its olive-trees. It is indeed a perfect

---

[1] Financier and philanthropist of German extraction (1865–1930).
[2] Jean Jules Jusserand (1855–1932), French writer and diplomat, who wrote in both French and English.

setting for a long afternoon of epicurean conversation – ideal for a sauntering dialogue.

On that platform I pace and hear – as I could hear from no one else in the world – the sort of details I love – about people in the Nineties – a perfect little portrait of Robert Buchanan – a celebrity whom oblivion has claimed (except for a column in the *D.N.B.*).[1]

14 April

After Max had ushered me out of the iron gate at the bottom of the steps (the gate was closed and I'd actually said good night) he delayed me another ten minutes – no delay ever more delightful – to say that he is within five pages of the end of the perusal of my book, which he has read 'with deep admiration' and intense interest. He found it 'poignant', and altogether he reassured my diffidence as to its merits.

On Friday night I wrote an alexandrine sonnet – addressed to Max – and finished it next day – in two two-hour periods of polishing (before lunch and after tea). An 'accomplished' piece of versifying – somewhat in the *Satirical Poems* technique, which I rarely practise now.

Memento for Max

Stored in my mind for life, these pacings on your roof,
These hours detached from brawling out-of-breath existence.
And in your 'social form' an amplitude of proof
That modernism delights me – at a decade's distance.
Delightful too (envisioned by Italian spring
And belvedered above a blandly sparkling sea)
To share your sheltered privacy of flowers, and bring
My gratitude for conversations yet to be.

But not for fumbling capture – what your talk retrieves
And conjures and evokes from late-Victorian rooms;
(Eminent phantoms, ghosts of genius, gifted shades).
And all your own, the effect – when fancy half believes
That while you make me laugh your voice invades
The elect who gather in Athenaeum-Olympian glooms.

---

[1] Poet, novelist and playwright (1841–1901), scourge of the Pre-Raphaelites.

Reading it now, I wonder how to make a prose-portrait of the *living* Max. He himself remarked yesterday that we all are made up of so many inconsistent selves that anything like an exact representation of them by a novelist would entirely bewilder the reader. He confessed that in spite of the continual opportunities he has had of getting to know himself, that knowledge is still very imperfect. 'Every morning I introduce myself to myself, and every night I tell myself that we have had a delightful day together, but the acquaintanceship remains experimental.' He had also remarked that fun is made of people who say that they 'know what they like', but to 'know what one likes' is really a very rare achievement. But to report (imperfectly) such remarks is not to reveal the living Max, since his writings are full of such observations, expressed in flawless and flexible prose.

20 April

I was in high spirits because, when I went up to Villino Chiaro after lunch to ask the M's to come here instead of me going there, Max talked a lot about my book, and gave it such praise that I was quite intoxicated. Mrs Max was equally impressed, and had written me a letter about it (which I shall always treasure as the first epistolary tribute to the book in its finished form).

30 April

And so we dined, and Max said that the best diarist he knows was B.R. Haydon.[1] I remained till midnight, blissfully occupied with Max, who went through my typescript and manuscript with me, offering a few helpful clarifications. This sent me home (manuscript under arm) feeling very happy about my book, and quite eager to revise the proofs. My manuscript is now embellished with a few pencillings by him – surely a very pleasant thing to contemplate. I don't know of anyone whose pencillings could please me more. Getting my manuscript back reminds me that I am in love with it (although it has seemed such weary work) and it makes me eager to begin another book.

Max's way of talking continually reminds me of dear Robbie

---

[1] Benjamin Robert Haydon, historical painter and diarist (1786–1846).

Ross[1] – I suppose it is the 'Bloomsbury voice' of the Nineties. They were great friends for a few years. Max's story of the drunken British tars at (pre-war) Rapallo – in the public gardens in evening – things getting beyond control – situation saved by Italian band-master at intervals striking up God Save the King – tars galvanized into temporary sobriety – standing rigidly to attention (Max illustrating this) and then lapsing into tipsiness again.

Tuesday [*12 July 1930*]   *23 Campden Hill Square*

Dear Max, I am in town for one night, and I long to see you. But I am so very sorry to hear that you are in such anxiety about your sister.[2] I have been at Wilsford[3] for several weeks. Stephen has been in bed, because of his lung-trouble. Yesterday a letter came from Sibyl Colefax,[4] proposing that she should motor you down to see Stephen, so I thought I had better find out whether you knew about this plan, as it seemed rather a strenuous day for you, and Stephen would so much like you to come and stay a week-end. But when I called at Apple Tree Yard this morning, the first thing I saw, at the foot of the stairs, was an envelope addressed to you in the well-known handwriting, so I knew that you are still unaware of your trip to Wiltshire (you could combine Stephen with Stonehenge, which is only two miles away).

I shall be dining at the Reform Club this evening. Could you possibly ring me up? I shall be there from 8 till 10.30 and would rush to any part of London for five minutes' conversation with you, dear Max. (Have we *ever* conversed for less than two hours?)

Yours ever   S.S.

10 December [*1930*]   *Great Western Royal Hotel, Paddington, W.2*

My dear Siegfried, I want to do a caricature of you – for the

---

[1] Robert Baldwin Ross (1869–1918). Literary journalist and art-critic. Dear friend of S.S. from 1915.
[2] Max's half-sister Constance (aged seventy-five) was about to undergo an operation in a nursing home.
[3] Stephen Tennant's home near Amesbury in Wiltshire.
[4] Relentless society hostess, died 1950.

Spectator. Do you mind? And are you in London? And, if not, shall you be so early next week? Do please send me a signal. Florence and I are at last definitely on the wing homeward.

Yours affectionately MAX BEERBOHM

P.S. I have, as a matter of fact, already done a rough drawing. But I want to 'check' it. I'm not sure that I have your colouring right.[1]

25 February 1931   *Great Western Hotel, Paddington*

My dear Siegfried, Yesterday, soon after seeing you, I went to a Private View of drawings and paintings by the very young Michael Rothenstein;[2] and Florence and I wished you were there too, to enjoy these things. I had seen only four or five of them; but there are about thirty of them; and they are very fine – very original and strong, with no nonsense about them – no Bloomsbury formalisation and arid mechanisation about them – and with genuine beauty throughout them. Do go and see them. (They are at the Warren Gallery, 19A Maddox Street.) And tell other people to do likewise.

Yours affectionately MAX BEERBOHM

29 April 1931   *Postcard from Hotel Monte Verita, Ascona*[3]

Hail to thee, blithe Spirit!
(Bard thou never wert.)
And here's our friend Sir Douglas Haig.
(A fly he wouldn't hurt.)   S.S.

I have just read Craig's *Irving* with immense enjoyment.[4]

[The postcard is a coloured portrait of Haig touched up by S.S.]

---

[1] Max and Florence went to tea with S.S. at 23 Campden Hill Square on 19 December, and the caricature appeared in a *Spectator* Supplement on 21 March 1931. All Max's caricatures were drawn from his superb visual memory, but occasionally he needed to check a detail, as in 1911 when he asked Reggie Turner to tell him the colour of D'Annunzio's hair.

[2] Painter and printmaker (born 1908). Younger son of Sir William.

[3] Near Locarno in Switzerland. S.S. stayed alone there from 30 March to 30 May 1931. His friend the composer William Walton was living near by.

[4] *Henry Irving* by Edward Gordon Craig (1930).

Max, you magician, how do you manage to make me want to be conversing with you, and make me want it so much? I am here alone. The Wyldes[2] are away in the South of France, and they invited me to stay with them in their absence – the Ideal Invitation: you ought to write a little essay 'On Staying with Absent Friends'. No one is so sociable as I am, when I am alone. And here I sit, keeping Schuster's memory green among his Leeds china, and perusing the advertisements in obsolete Guide Books. This morning I found a guide to Jeypore, a relic of Schuster's Durbar visit, and actually inscribed with the words 'H.E. Lady Curzon'. Did she give it to Frankie, or did he 'bone' it? The preface contains a good sentence. 'At the bottom of the street facing the Tripolia will be found a fine collection of tigers, most of which are said to have been man-eaters. Behind their cages, but reached from the road on the south of the city, are the Gas Works.'

Well, only a few hours ago I paid you a silent tribute, by placing Mrs Wylde's Lay Figure in an appropriately recumbent posture on a sofa. And now I have idly extracted a fat squat volume from the directory shelf. '*What's What: A Guide for to-day to life as it is and things as they are.* By Harry Quilter M.A.[3] 1902. Sonnenschein & Co.' (Sunshine & Co.) Much as I disapprove of the mutilation of other people's books, I (my thoughts flying to Villino Chiaro) tore out the frontispiece-portrait in a trice. So you can slip our old friend 'Arry into your copy of *The Gentle Art*, where it will remain as a silent allusion to one of our 'little' talks last year (and, more obviously, add to its interest as an 'extra-illustrated' copy).

It is six o'clock and a grey breezy day. The clock-winder has

---

[1] Frankie Schuster, wealthy music-lover and giver of parties (1840–1928). S.S. had often stayed with him at this house, which was first called The Hut and then The Long White Cloud.
[2] Schuster had left the house to his protégé Anzie Wylde and his artist wife Wendela.
[3] Art-critic (1851–1907), one of Whistler's *bêtes noires*.

just been in. Chatting with clock-winders once a week is a favourite pastime of mine.

I cannot quite see my way to the analogy, but I feel that some poet might well have written:

'If men could only wind the clock of Time
And make life last forever! But the hands
Move, and the world wears out their well-wound works.'

(Old Play)

I was about to start for Wilsford yesterday – from London – but a telegram put me off till Friday, Stephen being a little feverish. (He is much better lately.) So I came here instead, and have been feeling as though my mind were sitting still, after being out of breath since May 30, when I left Ascona and embarked on a five-weeks 'season' of Operas and Sitwells and asking old friends to luncheon at the Hyde Park Hotel. King Alfonso[1] was there one day, but he is not an old friend of mine and is unaware of my existence, although he has played polo with my relative Sir P.S.,[2] who, by the way, I met in Bumpus's bookshop recently, just off to the Berrr-litz School for a German lesson; does this mean that he will be obliged to know German at G.H.Q. in the next war? But I must conclude this chatter.

With love to the Pirandello Prima Donna[3] from   S.S.

Did you like *Pinchbeck Lyre?*[4] Unkind; but the result of much piffle-provocation.

[S.S. has pasted at the bottom of the page a coloured engraving of the Hotel Continental with the note 'Patronised by Max and other Crowned Heads'.]

---

[1] Alfonso XIII of Spain (1886–1941). Deposed 1931.

[2] S.S.'s distant cousin Sir Philip Sassoon (1888–1939) had been private secretary to Sir Douglas Haig 1915–18.

[3] Florence, who had played the leading part in Luigi Pirandello's one-act play *The Life I Gave You* at the Theatre Royal, Huddersfield, for a week from 4 May 1931.

[4] *Poems by Pinchbeck Lyre*, S.S. parodies of Humbert Wolfe's verse, was published anonymously on 15 May 1931.

[In type] This large-paper edition,
        printed on English hand-made
        paper, is limited to four
        hundred copies
           This is Number   20 October 1931

My dear Max, I saw something this afternoon. Let me tell you what it is. Perhaps you know already, for it is information which dates from 1909. (A nicer year than 'Nasty Nineteen Thirty-One'.)

It was only that I peeped into a little pamphlet in a bookshop. The pamphlet (24 mo) was 'anent' the funeral of G. Meredith. It began (and still begins) 'A few people were gathered about the gate' etc (of Box Hill). 'Mr Meredith was to be, as they say, buried. He had already been, as they say, cremated.' The authorship is obvious. ('The Great Sentimentalist'.)[1] 'I am suffering from, as they say, double-pneumonia.' 'Mr Beerbohm is, as they say, bankrupt.'

That is about all my news, except that I have lately – in an effort to evade 1931 – been making a small collection of Juvenile Books 1840–1875. I wish I could mount a magic carpet and bring them to lunch with you and Florence. Such elegant little coloured plates. Such innocent preceptorship. Perhaps in the future we may have something similar but different.

    Mama: 'Now Laura, dear, tell me whom you love most.'
    Laura: '*You*, Mama.'
    Mama: 'Hush, Laura. You must never say that! You must
            say "I love Lenin and Litvinoff".'
    Laura: 'But I *don't* love old Mr Lenin. And I hate this horrid
            bungalow. Papa says we used to live in a lovely park.
            When are we going back to it?'
    Mama: '*Never*, dear. It is unpatriotic to live in a park.'

But you need not be alarmed, my dear Max. No such regime is imminent. It is only my little joke. The Carlton Club will merely

---

[1] The quotations are from J.M. Barrie's article on George Meredith's funeral on 22 May 1909. It was reprinted in Barrie's *The Greenwood Hat* (1937).

call itself a 'Socialist Centre' and Christie's will be nationalized (with Lord MacDonald[1] as Minister of Old Masters).

Now I must close, with love to you both   S.S.

There was a rumour that Florence would be taking the stage again this winter. Please substantiate it.

P.S. I had an interesting letter from Lord Byron lately. Curiously enough, it seems to be written on the back of a sheet of paper on which some poetess has sent him a specimen of her verse. I enclose it. Throw it away when you have read it, as Lord B's letters are not worth keeping, though often lively.

21 February 1932   *Fitz House, Teffont Magna, Wilts.*[2]

My dear Max, I address this to you and not to Florence, though you don't deserve it, bless you. How I envy your capacity for epistolary idleness. I calculate that I concoct at least 365 unwilling replies per annum – but this, I regret to say, is not a *reply*, and it isn't unwilling. The truth is that last night I dreamt that I was dining with you. The first dish was – as far as I can recollect – something symbolising hard-boiled eggs. I ate mine without a word, and you did ditto. Then you said (with, I think, one of those engaging smiles of yours) 'How wise of you to eat such a good dish in silence.' This, I take it, was a Freudian intimation that I ought to communicate with you, and I am taking the opportunity to send you a copy of a little magazine in which I have lately become interested. The next number will be 'Reasons for not recommending Beerbohm as President of the Rugby Football Union of the United Kingdom'. Can you contribute?

Well, I have rented this old raftered and reconstructed residence for the winter and am more or less morose and singularly solitary in it.. Wilsford is exactly fourteen miles away. You will wish to hear some news of Stephen, so I will condense it for you (it is a tale which I am apt to enlarge on, with my 'long grey beard and

---

[1] James Ramsay MacDonald (1866–1937). Prime Minister, formerly of the first Labour Government, now of the National one.
[2] S.S. rented this house from October 1931 to January 1934.

glittering eye"[1]). He has made very little progress this winter, and has been in bed since October. His illness has become an obsession with him, and he will see no one. I suppose that such a monotonous existence has made him feel that the easiest way is to shut his eyes; and he has become so low in mental aliveness, through lack of nutrition from other minds, that anything in the nature of an idea tires him. Even orchids over-excite him, he announced recently, and he is sick and tired of arum lilies. No one can persuade him to make an effort to be less lethargic, because he refuses to take any suggestion of any kind, and rules his nurses and doctor inflexibly. Five weeks ago he had a haemorrhage, but it doesn't seem to have been a serious symptom, though it has caused him to exist in a sort of vacuum of carefulness ever since. I fear that he will soon have become, in the minds of his friends, a pressed flower between the pages of a book of memory. But he could never be moderate in anything he did; and as at least half of me is always loitering about in his locality waiting for him to get well, I am not an impartial judge of his methods of enduring this dreadful illness. But if only we could do something to help him! Obstinate little creature that he is! O that we two were Maying[2] (at Villino Chiaro). But *nil desperandum*, as the classical scholars say.

I must be gay; though 'By Gum, I usually feel about as jolly as a prairie-oyster', as some Yankee humorist might say.

By the way, I came across a book entitled *Fifty Years Correspondence, Inglish, French, and Lattin, in Proze and Verse, between Geniusses ov boath Sexes*. This was by a certain James Elphinston (1721–1809), and he thus anticipated the late Laureate[3] by over a hundred years. He wrote a long poem called 'Education', in which he uses the word 'adscititious' – a word which fairly sticks in the gullet.

In a *Poetical Register* (1811) I discovered the following touching stanzas, by the Rev. Robert Graves:

> 'My life's prolonged full many a year
> Beyond life's usual space;

---

[1] Coleridge, 'The Rime of the Ancient Mariner'.
[2] Charles Kingsley, 'The Saint's Tragedy'.
[3] Robert Bridges (1844–1930). A keen advocate of spelling reform.

Yet, ah! in that long life, I fear,
Heaven few good deeds can trace.
But, as I've cherished in my breast
A love of all mankind,
I may, 'tis hoped, among the blest
An humble mansion find.'

My nearest neighbour in this village is called Colonel Kennedy Shaw. I fear I must class him with Dr Fell. But he informed me that he was in the same House at Charterhouse with M. Beerbohm. What was he like? I queried artlessly. 'There was something sarcastic about him, even as a boy.' 'Can you *away* with Wordsworth?' he asked, seeing that I had a volume of W. on my table. 'Do you know that line of his, "A Mr Wilkinson, a clergyman"?' he continued. (Drat the man, I thought, why I knew that that line was by Tennyson or one of his set, before I was fourteen!).[1] 'Also,' I felt inclined to say, 'I do not require to be reminded that Wordsworth was deficient in humour.' How withering! But I permitted the poor man to depart in peace ... 'Beerbohm sarcastic, indeed!' Tush! Anyhow I must conclude this before you re-echo my ejaculation (tush).

And stands the dear old Bristol where it stood?
And is Rapallo's climate just as good?
Strolls philosophic Beerbohm on his roof,
Exclaiming, when the weather's sultry, 'Poof'?
From affectionate old S.S.

[S.S. first saw Hester Gatty at the Wilton Pageant on 9 June 1933. They met by chance in September and after a whirlwind courtship were married on 18 December. They lived at Fitz House until 26 January 1934, when they left for a honeymoon tour by ship to Spain, Sicily and Italy, where at the end of April they spent a fortnight at the Hotel Bristol at Rapallo. No description of their stay is recorded in S.S.'s diary. They arrived back in England on 16 May, and two days later moved into their new home, Heytesbury

---

[1] It was a parody of Wordsworth by Edward FitzGerald.

House, near Warminster in Wiltshire. S.S. lived there for the rest of his life.]

27 April [*1935*]   *Heytesbury House, Wiltshire*

My dear Max, This envelope which you have just opened has been in my writing-table drawer 'for many moons' (as some Irish bard might put it) and all the time it contained Desmond's article.[1] But I thought (as the late G. Moore might say) that perhaps Max is sick of the aroma of 'Yeats *et tous ces autres*', and the envelope stayed where it was. I have now changed my mind, and I can't help feeling that, after all, Max *may* be amused. Dear old 'Willie' is such an irresistible attraction to my irreverent tendency. I have now discovered a few lines which I once scribbled in Willie's last volume of verse:

He begins to doubt their Authenticity

I fiddled to the fair at Ballyhinch.
Blind Fergus gave me sixpence for my lunch;
But *Old Moore's Almanac* I bought instead.
That afternoon I drank the Liffey dry
And dreamed of gold and lapis lazuli
While seven white symbols perched upon my head.
Rich men, says Burke, have lost their large estates
(What price the works of W.....m B....r Y...s?)

Well, Max, it's no use me and Hester wishing you were here (as we often do) because you aren't. All we can do is to send our best love to you and Florence. I read *Zuleika* again last winter; it is a rattling good book, and you seem to have quite a sense of style. (It is absolutely *perfect*.)   Yours ever   S.S.

---

[1] Probably Desmond MacCarthy's long review in the *Sunday Times* of W.B. Yeats's volume of plays *Wheels and Butterflies* (November 1934).

P.S. The picture whose rejection caused me to resign from the Academy.

St Francis Feeding the Birds

17 May 1935   *Heytesbury*

My dear Max, Allow me to say – just *once* more – that you *are* my favourite author (and artist). As for the enclosed letter, I feel that you will share my delight in its mastery of the reporter-cliché technique. The whole thing is such glorious bosh.

I long to discuss the Silver Jubilee[1] with you (not in a spirit of mockery, for it was all very kindly and genuine, I think, and has, I am sure, 'done the "Old Country" a power of good'). Hester and I 'listened in' to Kipling's speech,[2] which was most extraordinary. He spoke with fanaticism in his voice, like a suave precise professor of military law, also like a prophet who has been disregarded for a decade and a half and was taking his chance to get his own back. Hester and I sat there feeling almost frightened by his intensity, but we decided afterwards that modern European nations aren't Old Testament tribes, and that Kipling was exaggerating a bit.

We are feeling very sad about the poor 'Aircraftsman', but there seems a faint hope that he may recover.[3] This morning I received a letter from the *Observer* asking me to write a 'personal appreciation' ('in the unfortunate event of the accident proving fatal'). How *does* one do that sort of writing, I wonder.

The 'modern world' is rather awful, isn't it – but one can contrive to evade the shindy by escaping into one's own world, and I can do that very well here, in this lovely place with sweet Hester to help.

'*Quelle – salle – magnifique*', as I remarked the other day when entering our dining-room. With love to you both   S.S.

Silver Jubilee Celebration[4]
(At the Dinner of the Royal Society of St George)

Broadcast across the as yet unbeaconed dark,
I heard the shout of that symposiarch
Whose voice, like some Gargantuan-mouthed grotesque,
Demanded silence for the honoured guest.

---

[1] Of King George V and Queen Mary on 6 May 1935.
[2] To the Royal Society of St George on 6 May 1935.
[3] T.E. Lawrence, who was fatally injured in a motor-cycle accident on 13 May 1935, and died on 19 May.
[4] There is no proof that S.S. sent this poem to Max, but he may well have done. It was published in his *Rhymed Ruminations* (1940).

Then – when prolonged applauding had subsided –
Kipling, that legendary name, confided
In us – a host of atmospheric ears –
His planned post-mortem on the post-war years.

Suavely severe – not one bleak syllable blurred –
In dulcet-bitter and prophetic tones
(Each word full charged with dynamite deferred)
He disinterred a battlefield of bones . . .
And then reminded us that our attempt
To put all war behind us with the last one
Had been a dream administrators dreamt;
In fact a virtuous fallacy — and a vast one.

Meanwhile his audience, mystified at first,
Sat spellbound while he preached with barbed conviction,
Who, through implied anathemas, re-cursed
Our old opponents in that four-years friction.
And if indeed it was the astringent truth
He told with such incomparable concision –
That we must now re-educate our youth
With 'Arm or Perish' as their ultimate vision—

Let us at least be candid with the world
And stitch across each Union Jack unfurled
'No bargain struck with Potsdam is put over
Unless well backed by bombers – and Jehovah!'

29 December 1935   *Heytesbury*

My dear Max, I have got out my pen and paper – in my old-fashioned way! – to 'write' and tell you how much we (Mr and Mrs S. Sassoon, a quiet couple living in the country) enjoyed your – er – 'Talk'.[1]

It seems rather strange now, when I think that you were really addressing – not me and Hester while wearing a cloak of invisibility, but the 'contemporary situation' (as the current phrase goes). And

---

[1] Max's first broadcast, 'London Revisited', on 29 December 1935.

how beautifully you did it. I felt as if I were listening to the voice of the last 'civilised man' left on earth.

'What an amusing man Mr Beerbohm must be!' exclaims the outer world, opening up the card-table and shuffling the packs for a few quiet rubbers of bridge. 'Has he written books?' asks the dealer, adding 'Three clubs'. (Brooks's, Boodles, and White's?)

'Who *is* this guy Beerbohm?' asks a business man in a service-flat in Dorchester House. 'Never heard of him,' replies his friend, who is a director of the Acropolis Ferro-Concrete Company, adding 'bloody near actionable – what he said about modern buildings.'

'How divine Max is,' enunciated Lady Desborough to the Lord High Almoner, who replied 'Most amusin' man – capital speaker.' (But he felt that somehow his leg had been pulled, though he couldn't put his finger on the place.)

'It suggested Aristophanes,' chanted Willie Yeats (he didn't know why, but it sounded impressive).

What *I* say is that it was a triumphal success, and I adored every word of it, and felt the wisdom of the ages in it, and the glory of exquisite art and the affirmation of exquisite courtesy. Everything was there which I love and value deeply. It was 'the real right thing',[1] as far as I was concerned.

But then, you see – it was you, Max – and you always do things perfectly. The BBC is your footstool and your hand is stretched out over Fleet Street.

I am still working at my book, which is almost almost finished.[2] Is there any danger of your leaving England before I can see you?

S.S.

29 May 1936   *Heytesbury*

My dear Max, My attempt to talk to you on the telephone in town yesterday was thwarted by your lamented absence 'in the country' – 'O that we two were Maying', I muse; but maugre the fact that we aren't (what a thistle of a word *maugre* is!) I still hope that we

---

[1] Henry James, in his story of that name.
[2] *Sherston's Progress*, published on 3 September 1936.

may 'meet and make merry in unmalignèd mirth' – as some poet probably says somewhere. Dare we suggest that you and Florence visit Heytesbury toward the close of June? Or will you be too busy getting in the hay and herding your munching kine?

I have just been reading the list of the members of the Savage Club (which I have been invited to join, but shall not do so for reasons of my own) and I couldn't help wishing that your next year's Academy picture might be 'Saturday Night at the Savage Club – January 1st 1900'.

This morning I met Lord Berners[1] in the Green Park. He was in high spirits, and told me that one of the exhibits at the forthcoming Surrealist Exhibition is to be 'a tea-set of squirrels' fur'. He urged me to exhibit something. Shall I do a bust of you – in thistledown? (symbolising your inimitable lightness of touch). The verses which I enclose were written last autumn, but I refrained from sending them to you, feeling that our old friend of (or is it *in*) the Charterhouse might be a fatiguing subject for you to be reminded of. But now I am hoping that you will 'It with a tolerant eye perhaps peruse, And not the tribute of a smile refuse'.

After all this persiflage I dare not say anything serious – except *please come and stay with us this summer*. With love from us both to you both   S.S.

'The Real Zuleika Dobson'[2]

Quoth Graves, 'It is my proper field
To make the world's best books read bleaker.
I've dealt with *David Copperfield*;
And I will now re-write *Zuleika*'.

His pencil (blue) he thus employed,
Deleting what we'd all enjoyed;
And at the end felt shocked and pained
To find that not one word remained.

---

[1] Gerald, fourteenth Lord Berners (1883–1950), composer, painter, writer.
[2] *The Real David Copperfield*, Robert Graves's rewriting of the novel, was published in March 1933. Like Max, Graves had been to school at Charterhouse.

[S.S. did not keep a regular diary in 1936, but he recorded that Max and Florence were at Heytesbury from 10 to 17 July, and on 18 July he noted: 'Max being here made it seem like living in a delightful book – living in a harmoniously working mind, as it were.']

19 July 1936   *41 Tavistock Square, W.C.1*

Dearest Hester and Siegfried, Needless to say, Florence and I have been thinking and talking about you all the time, and about our lovely visit. This morning I said to Florence, 'They are both of them lovely spirits, in a lovely' – and here I paused for the right word, and could only think of 'bottle', and *said* 'bottle', and then righted myself and spoke the word I had wanted 'setting'; which Florence thought a great improvement.

Heytesbury is indeed worthy of you. I doubt whether any other place would be. But do let Rapallo be a temporary rival – and *soon*!
Your affectionate   MAX

[*Telegram, Postmark 31 October 1936*]

HESTER HAS A SON   BOTH WELL
SIEGFRIED

31 October [*1936*]   *Villino Chiaro, Rapallo*

My dear dear Hester and Siegfried, This was indeed glorious and joyful news. The telegraph boy, who saw me open the telegram, said 'Ah, I am so glad you have good news, *signora*', for in my joy I jumped up and down and clapped my hands. I have been anxious and so yearning to hear, but I knew that so many people were anxious and yearning that it wasn't right to tell you of my yearning.

I long to know everything, but what we do know is very much and I shall wait patiently to hear more, only sending you all now my fond love – and every wish for your happiness and for the dear child all the happiness it deserves as the child of Hester and Siegfried. Could I wish it more?   Lovingly   FLORENCE

31 October 1936   *Villino Chiaro, Rapallo*

Dearest Siegfried, Love to all three of you! I know well that two
of you are the salt of the earth, and I am sure that the third one
is too – and that Hester's and your firm conviction that he *is* will
be no mere fond illusion, but a lovely fact. The child of such
parents cannot help being adorably rather more and very much
more than all right.

What will he be christened? Sherston? Or Hesterus? Or what?
But names are very unimportant: it's the bearer that makes the
name, in due time. With love again,   Your affectionate   MAX

10 November 1936   *18 Hanover Terrace, N.W.1*[1]

MY DEAR MAX, I can't continue this WILLOWY calligraphy to which
the spirit of creativeness has moved me. Not the least like Mr
Dombey, I overhear the voice of infant George Thornycroft Sassoon in the upper regions, while I sit in the structural equivalent
of Edmund and Nellie Gosse's drawing-room, lacking, alas, their
selves, and those Japanese prints and the picture of – was it apple-
blossom – by Alfred Parsons.[2] Listening also, about an hour ago,
to the – to me – rather raucous voice of the Prime Minister warning the world from the Guildhall, I wondered whether you also
listened.

> I wonder, were you listening too? –
> Uttering a hushed 'bravo' or 'pooh'.

Meanwhile Hester, thank heaven, is well. 'George is in cradle; all's
well with the world.' What cares he for 'international questions'?
He doesn't even care when he will be christened.* Even his pram
is as yet *terra incognita* to him.

---

[1] The Sassoons rented this house from 7 October till 30 November, so that their
child could be born there. The Gosses lived at No 17.
[2] Painter and book-illustrator (1847–1920).

What cares he for the Albert Hall
And speeches by Dick Sheppard?[1]
What cares he if Nazis all
By Bolshie bullets be peppered?
And what care I if Mr Eden
Our Colonies will be concedin'?
Ah, well might Florence leap for joy
To hear of Heyt'sb'rys newborn boy!

Query: does this letter, so far, sound like the ordered utterance of a responsible parent?

I must now tell you that little George is very like his papa. He has the same face, but his eyes are at present a good deal darker. He weighs seven and a half pounds and is twenty-two inches long. His nurse describes him as one of the calmest babies she has known, though very vigorous. Will he, I wonder, become Prime Minister, Poet Laureate, Archbishop of Canterbury, or merely Editor of the *Times Literary Supplement?* – or Master of the Quorn? Or merely the Squire of Heytesbury? (In my opinion the latter is preferable to all else.)   With much love from us all   S.S.

* (But he *might* care to know that the names of Max and Florence Beerbohm have been – without permission – included among his godfathers and godmothers.)

17 November [*1936*]   *Villino Chiaro, Rapallo*

My dear Hester, You and Siegfried will know how happy and proud Siegfried's letter made us and how eager we are for all the dear news. As for our future grandeur we are impressed by our importance and greatly gratified and we only hope that little George, when he gets a little older, will not be bewildered and wonder why you chose us for our part of the godmother and godfathership. We shall try to convince him that we have something that will explain much. We begin by loving him. Our fond love

FLORENCE

---

[1] The Rev. H.R.L. Sheppard (1880–1937). Vicar of St Martin-in-the-Fields 1914–27. Pacifist and founder of the Peace Pledge Union. Canon of St Paul's from 1934.

17 November 1936   *Villino Chiaro, Rapallo*

Dearest Siegfried, What an enchanting letter! So full of so many
qualities – with happiness bubbling up especially all over them. It
is lovely to think of you and Hester and George together, next
door to the dear Gosses, under that familiar arcade, with people
able to look straight in through the dining-room window, and the
canal flowing so slowly and decently through the (I hope not-
quite-built-over) park.

But there's nothing like Heytesbury – though Rapallo is a
passable substitute for it during the month of March, I hope. What
a joy it will be to see you both! – and to see you three later on.

Your affectionate   MAX G.G.*

* a godfather of George.

21 November 1936   *18 Hanover Terrace*

My dear Max and Florence – How odd if your names were Maurice
and Fleurette!

But a truce to this persiflage!

George and Hester are thriving and we are all a mutual admiration society – my share of the prestige being the fact that I
resemble George, whose already adorably expressive countenance
takes the resemblance for granted. I just mentioned to him that
his leading godfather is a Litt.D. of Edinburgh; he looked a bit
glum till I murmured 'Edinburgh Rock' whereupon he smiled
sweetly. Yesterday he celebrated his twenty-first sunset; and I
celebrated my first appearance on the Peace Pledge Platform.

(General Goering hasn't yet wired 'Gratters', but no doubt he is grateful.) On November 27 I reappear at the Albert Hall to ask 8500 people if they have 'forgotten yet'[1] in stentorian tones. I am wondering what the effect would be if I gave my reading in my pseudo Major Paget voice.[2] I have just tried 'Everyone Sang' on Hester, and she laughed so much that I got quite nervous. (The Major put in a parenthesis after the first verse, in which he recalled the high birds which he used to 'bring down' when they were winging wildly across the woods of Plâs Paget.) But I fear that dear Dick Sheppard wouldn't approve of a 'Paget reading'. At Birmingham there were 3000 people in the Town Hall, and 2000 at an overflow meeting, so it was quite a beano of Quakers. But is it any more illogical than world-behaviour as a whole? Much less, if only there weren't so many dictators. Anyhow my poems are very effective when read, which is more than can be said for many of those included in Willie Yeats's anthology[3] (seventeen pages of W.J. Turner and sixteen of Lady Gerald Wellesley, three of Hardy and two of S.S.!) – which reminds me that Willie's National Broadcast on poetry[4] was a most extraordinary performance – it sounded like a burlesque and must have put several million people 'off' poetry for ever! As usual, he was very strong on *swans*, and I composed a couplet:

> Where one wan swan upon a dim pond swam
> Sat Butler Yeats – that grand old Irish ham.

Anyhow George is to be baptised by Dick Sheppard at St Martin-in-the-Fields on November 28. It ought to be a gay ceremony. 'Come on chaps' etc. How happy lovely Hester will be.

With much love from us both   S.S.

---

[1] The first line of S.S.'s poem 'Aftermath'.

[2] Major George Thomas Cavendish Paget (1859–1939), grandson of the first Marquess of Anglesey. A great clubman and a soldier of fortune. In the Boer War he raised a force of gentlemen rankers and officers called Paget's Horse (known in South Africa as Piccadilly Heroes or Perfectly Harmless). Presumably he had lived or stayed at Rapallo, where Max and S.S. had known him.

[3] *The Oxford Book of Modern Verse* (1936).

[4] *Modern Poetry*, broadcast on 11 October 1936, published as a pamphlet in December.

Asked whether he's seen Eliot's poetical play about Becket, Mr Joe Beckett, former heavy-weight boxer, denied any knowledge of either. The only poem he'd ever read was 'Two Lovely Black Eyes'.

Famous Irish bard Yeats admits that swan is his favourite bird. Is considering writing a 'Swannet' Sequence and has been made an honorary Writer to the Cygnet.

Recent *mot* by epigrammatiste Princess Bibesco.[1] Inquired for opinion of Peace Pledge Union, she replied that it 'wouldn't *paix*'.

'Simple Souls'

or

How HEYTESBURY HOUSE WILTSHIRE behaved during the Constitutional Crisis[2]

14 December 1936

Scene i Arrival of two vans containing Hester's share of the furniture from Lady St Cyres's[3] London house. Sheltie dissuaded from biting feet of men carrying tables and chairs and trophies into front hall. Hall becomes congested with settees, arm-chairs, and lovely lacquer cupboards etc. Two large solid-lead gilt ornaments trundled in. Query: ought we to offer them to Stonehenge. Hester concerned about their heaviness. Might they not fall on George when old enough to trip over them? Departure of vans and men in green baize aprons, full of beer.

Scene ii Arrival of men from Warminster to hang pictures and

---

[1] Novelist daughter of Henry and Margot Asquith (1897–1945). Wife of Prince Antoine Bibesco.

[2] That which culminated in the abdication of King Edward VIII on 11 December.

[3] Dorothy (née Morrison), widow of Viscount St Cyres (1869–1926), only son of the second Earl of Iddesleigh. Her husband died a year before his father, so never succeeded to the earldom. She died 1936.

hoist furniture about. Lacquer 'pieces' nicely arranged in garden-hall and small drawing-room. I agree that it looks perfect (and plead for no revolutionary alterations to the music-room – being a creature of habit) . . . An hour elapses during which I feel terribly sorry for poor little King Edward; try to feel tolerant about Mrs Simpson; and assume that the nicest possible feelings prevail throughout the country – about the whole business . . . Loud rumblings from the garden-hall and small drawing-room. I return to find Hester re-arranging everything. We agree that it is a great improvement. But how *are* we to dispose of those seven high-backed and highly uncomfortable painted monastic chairs. No private chapel on the premises, so we put them, pro-visionally, into the – ahem – lavatory, where they look quite nice. Wireless announces that Mrs Simpson has gone to the South of France. We can't help *hoping* that she will remain there. Seriously scrutinizing three photos of her in the *Tatler*, we come to the conclusion that she is too unlike Queen Mary to be made to look appropriate on the Throne. 'Can it be possible' – we query – that she is 'an adventuress'? . . . We suppress the notion as unworthy of our better selves, and I nearly put my foot through an eighteenth-century Dutch picture which is half-reclining against an ultra-rococo console-table with its legs in the air. *Happy thought*. Put that pew-like red velvet sofa in front of the library fireplace. Good place to hide from callers in! Perfect place for Max to compose broadcasts in, too – or better still – for him to recline in and look at life-sized Academy portrait of Mrs Beer[1] (in 1888) which now hangs above fireplace. How charming she looks, with huge feather fan and not a scrap of jewellery on ('What a pity Mrs Simpson doesn't look more like that'; one can't repress the thought).

Scene iii   King still making up his mind at Fort Belvedere. Every-

---

[1] Mrs Rachel Beer (1858–1927), S.S.'s father's sister.

one praying that he will do the right thing and be influenced by consulting Mr Baldwin – 'rather than the bottle', a cynic might add. George's nannie, who used to be with the Haigs (of Ypres), feels dubious whether she wants the Yorks on the Throne. Holding up a heavy picture for Hester to see 'how it would look in that corner', I make a feeble joke about Masefield's 'Simpson Agonistes'. No gossip reaches us from the 'great world' and there is a thick fog. Hester's brother rings up from London to say that Bernard Shaw has written an article advocating a morganatic marriage. Could this be constitutionally organatic? we wonder.

Scene iv   All eyes on Fort Belvedere. We begin to feel that some of the new furniture will have to be given away. I keep bumping into things, and have always preferred undercrowding. Have decided to cancel my Harley Street appointment with the dentist on December 10. In the teeth of such national suspense I hardly feel equal to having a wisdom tooth stopped. BBC announcers become more momentous in their enunciations of the phrase 'His Majesty', but he is still making up his – one assumes – extremely human mind. Shall we see a headline in *The Times* – 'Lady Colefax sees the King'? Nothing would surprise my innocent mind – the situation being what it is! Wonder what Major Paget thinks about it all. Hester unable to decide whether we ought to use superb blue-and-gold Spode tea and coffee service left her by Lady St Cyres. I suggest wait till Max and Florence come to stay, as maids smashed all the eggshell coffee-cups since Edward VIII's accession.

Scene v   George brought down to music-room so that his nannie can hear 'Prince Edward' broadcast his explanation of recent odd behaviour. Hester's verdict, 'He didn't *sound* like a gentleman.'

Scene vi   Edith Olivier[1] to tea. Spate of stories from well-informed

---

[1] Writer (1879–1948). She lived at The Daye House, Quidhampton, Salisbury, and was a good friend to S.S.

circles. We are no longer innocent. Mrs S. now regarded as adventuress, and heartfelt relief expressed about Yorks being now in charge of Empire. Hester quite sure that George knows me by sight, which is more than can be said about George VI.

21 *March 1937*   *Heytesbury*

Palm Sunday (St Gratuity's Day – a joke)

My dear – Florence (*yes*; *not* Max, that non-epistolary pseudo-Paget). So far this letter looks more like a bit of algebra than an announcement of the (I hope) delightful news that we intend to leave for 'the Bristol' on April 6th, and rely on your usual angelic assistance in tipping the manageress the wink that we shall require the Royal Suite plus something in the nature of a sitting-room (though we hope not to sit in it very often, unless you and Max come and sit with us).

Before I forget, are there any recently published books that we can 'bring out'? I had thought of bringing Trevelyan's *Grey* and Coward's autobiography[1] – a contrast – in case Max cared to glance his eye at them. But are there any others? Not many, I imagine. I must now break the news that Max will be requested to read 27,500 words which I have been copying out in a blue-buckram-bound manuscript-book for the last two months. It is (or they are) the first eight chapters of my life – up to 1897.[2] Personally I think them very enjoyable reading, and Hester of course considers them a combination of Shakespeare and Turgenev. Anyhow the warning has been given and I hope for the best – and for many a helpful hint from the senior writer. Alas, that we cannot bring George, who, though I say it with blatant parental pride, is more adorable every day. His spontaneous smiles and vocalised squeaks reduce us to infatuated rapture, and when he holds up his hands toward his dangled beads he looks like a little poet. He does everything with such intensity. 'Nothing lackadaisical about Master George'

---

[1] *Grey of Falloden* by G.M. Trevelyan and *Present Indicative* by Noel Coward (both 1937).
[2] *The Old Century and Seven More Years* (1938).

36

is the generally expressed opinion. But this is mere boasting! ...
Roll on April 7th, say we.   With love from   S.S.
I think we are coming by the train which one changes from at
Ventimiglia.

Siegfried's 1937 Diary

6 April (midnight)   *Rapallo, Excelsior Hotel*

Left Victoria 1 p.m. yesterday. Smooth crossing. Arrived here
about noon (watch put on an hour). Max and Florence met us at
the station and brought us up here to show us the rooms F. had
engaged, which are spacious and cheerful (much better than the
Hotel Bristol). Last time I stayed at this hotel was in November
1929, when the weather was bad and I got an impression that the
hotel was gloomy. I gave Max the manuscript of my book. At 7
we went to Villino Chiaro for dinner, and stayed till 10.15. Max
had already read about a third of my manuscript and is liking it
very much, quite fulfilling my hopes about it.

When we went from the dining-room to the next room I found
that I'd forgotten about the Walter Greaves painting of Swinburne
and Rossetti walking along Chelsea Embankment.[1] Had I tried
to visualise the room yesterday I should have remembered the
Harlequin picture[2] but not the Greaves, though I've admired it
fifty times in the past. The engraving of George IV in the dining-
room also took me by surprise – as unremembered, though familiar
once I saw it there. This shows the importance of putting things on
paper if one wants to recover a background accurately afterwards. (I
intend to make a lot of notes this time.)

Maxiana

17 Hanover Terrace was the home of Wilkie Collins's father.
Dickens met J.E. Millais there (after his attack on 'Christ in the

---

[1] Although signed with Greaves's name, this picture was in fact painted by Max.
It is now in the Max Room at Merton College, Oxford.
[2] By Mabel Pryde, the first wife of William Nicholson.

House of his Parents').[1] Gosse didn't know about the Collinses having lived there until Max told him.

The Archbishop of Canterbury's broadcast after the abdication. 'Supreme moral courage needed to kick a man when he is down.' (But Max agreed with the Archbishop, on the whole.)

M. on Virginia Woolf (too luminous).
M. on H.G.W. 'The future; not interesting because we don't know what it will be like. Some scientist has suggested that with the decrease of population half of England in 300 years will be "defectives".' Futility of H.G's 1900 idea that if carefully selected people of all nations could only 'get together' and thrash things out etc in thirty years the world would be peaceful and prosperous. 'Great story-teller but no prophet.'

I told M. that R. Graves had got a £12,000 film contract with Mr Korda. M. 'He should now write "How do you do to All This"!'

8 April (10.45 p.m.)

Fine weather yesterday and today. Did nothing yesterday. Read ninety pages of Virginia Woolf's *The Years* after dinner. (Rather a mechanical performance – no real life in it, though very well written.)

Lunched at Villino Chiaro today. There 12.30–6. Max had been prevented from continuing my manuscript (which he referred to as 'The Enchantment') yesterday, so discussion of it is delayed.

But how lovely it was to be jogging up the hill in a horse-carriage with the charm of Italian gardens below and above the road – flowers overhanging wistariaed walls, fig-trees coming into leaf, cypress-spires against the sea – rich young grass in orchards – till we drew up outside the Villino – and went through the narrow double iron gates in the arched doorway in the wall and up the stone steps to be greeted by Max leaning over the parapet of his platform. And then to go up more steps and be on that platform

---

[1] In *Household Words* on 15 June 1850 Dickens described this painting by Millais as 'mean, odious, revolting and repulsive'. Later he became a great friend and admirer of Millais. The picture belonged to S.S.'s aunt Rachel before it was bought by the Tate Gallery (see S.S.'s *1920–22 Diaries*, p. 234).

of flat roof, with the sea far below – to be above the world with Max in his exquisite detachment (his little familiar room up there regularising his mind, as it were). Behind it, in the garden, the little crooked-stemmed cherry-tree in white blossom – flattened branches – a Japanese drawing of a tree, it looked, civilised and 'stylised'. The large earthenware pots with camellia-trees in them (no flowers yet) and the sun-bleached wicker chairs which Max so seldom sits down on – and Florence bringing out the big umbrella on its stand.

A shower of rain after lunch, when we'd been sitting there for a bit, so we moved on to the Casetta[1] room, and had tea there. Max, as usual, taking no tea, but only a glass of white wine from the large flask which the white-overalled Italian maid places on the table for him. All just the same as it was three years ago, except, alas, that M. is three years older (though, if possible, a richer talker). The bread-and-butter and cakes brought in with muslin over them for fly-protection. Florence lighting an unneeded wood-fire which crackles cheerfully until the room is a little too hot. The old upright piano in the corner, and Mrs William Nicholson No 1's little picture of the harlequin in the other corner above the bookcase by the door.

Max making us laugh ecstatically with an imitation of an Austrian Rothschild talking about the Duke of Windsor,[2] or momentarily impersonating the late Duke of Marlborough (and somehow making himself look like a horsey little ineffective ducal bounder). When M. imitates someone he seems to alter his face; his whole personality changes. He is an incomparable mimic. Hester and I walked home (delicious evening after the rain).

10 April (11 a.m.)

Grey weather this morning; soft wind from the sea – scirocco – but not unpleasant. Yesterday was perfect weather. Quietly spent day, and I went for a nice walk up the hill-paths above San Michele, 5.30–7. Max and Florence came to dinner, and we sat

---

[1] A cottage above the terrace.
[2] The Duke stayed with Baron Eugene de Rothschild at Schloss Enzesfeld, near Vienna, while waiting for Mrs Simpson's divorce to be made absolute.

Max and Florence

talking at the table for one-and-a-half hours. Max has finished
reading my manuscript and the result is a triumph. He says 'it is
a perfectly lovely thing' – 'like going out into a garden at 6 o'clock
on a summer morning!' 'You have put the dewy cobwebs and
dewdrops on to the paper without breaking a single dewdrop. You
have shown childhood as it seemed to a child.' He added, rather
ruefully, 'and of course it will be an *enormous* success in England
and America, and then, dear Siegfried, I shall feel that I don't
want to know you any more!' – by which, of course, he meant that
he hated the idea of my delicate performance being vulgarised –
and *how* I agree with him! He said it is the best writing I have
done.

After dinner Hester and I were introduced to the Hauptmanns
(Gerhart[1] and his wife and their son Benvenuto) and we conversed
till 11.30, sitting round two little tables in the bar and sipping red

---

[1] German dramatist and novelist (1862–1946). Awarded the Nobel Prize 1912.

Chianti and soda-water. Old Hauptmann speaks no English, and Max and I no German, but Mrs H. talks good English, and so does the son. M. and I talked to Mrs H. while Florence talked to G.H., and Hester listened to Benvenuto, who filled her head with stories about the National Socialist Government in Germany (which is, he asserted, unpopular now, and not likely to last when Hitler dies. Hitler has cancer in the throat, he said). Meanwhile I gazed appreciatively at old Hauptmann. He wears a long square-cut black frock-coat, the waistcoat buttoned up to the neck, just showing a loose tie – giving an effect of clerical costume. His fine head with white hair grown long and brushed up far back from his immense brow. A lot of delicately pencilled lines above the eyebrows – the rest of his face fleshy and healthy and pink, without any wrinkles. The eyes rather small and wise-looking. He speaks slowly and deliberately, looking almost too obviously 'a great man' – I kept thinking of Liszt – 'the Abbé Hauptmann' was how I saw him. (I must observe his *hands* next time.) He seemed a kindly old-fashioned German – the 'good old Germany' was sitting there. At the beginning he raised his glass and said to me, very slowly (in German) 'We both serve the same masters – Art and Literature.' It was most charming, the way this fine old poet did it. Altogether an evening of complete enjoyment. (I showed them George's photograph, which was much admired for 'the look of intelligence in the eyes'.)

Joke about 'Parsifal Griffiths' – an old gent, with white hair and a beautiful 'lady friend', who the Hauptmanns thought was me – having been told so by the barman! Max produced his matchbox (given to Ellen Terry by Stephen Coleridge, and to M. by Gordon Craig). It has on it Mr William Shakespeare, Stratford-on-Avon, like a visiting-card.

12 April (12.30 p.m.)

Better weather yesterday. To Villino for tea (there 4-6.30), Max reading P.G. Wodehouse's *Summer Lightning* – which I'd lent him – with much relish. He was wearing his almost-white tweed suit and buff cloth spats and a stiff-brimmed hat with a stiff round crown (an American army hat which Florence's brother gave him). Florence looked her best in her moss-green corduroy-velvet dress

Siegfried and the Beerbohms at Rapallo

buttoned up to the throat, which suits her silvery hair – still pale gold above the forehead. Max gave us imitations of Swaffer[1] broadcasting, and Austen Chamberlain[2] conversing in parliamentary style. (Via *The Initials*[3] – Hildegarde, the heroine – an old novel much admired by Joe Chamberlain. Arthur Balfour also remembered having liked it, but couldn't remember the heroine's name – a good story which showed the contrast between J.C. and A.J.B.) Neville Chamberlain, he said, talks quite naturally in private. Reminds him a little of George Wyndham[4] – 'eyes like an intellectual dog'. Gave us a good Shorter[5] imitation. (Robertson Nicoll[6] giving a lunch for Hardy at the Devonshire Club, with Shorter there.) Meredith and Hardy, he said, put up with Shorter's posturings because they thought he was an influential critic; they didn't realise that the day of influential reviews was over by 1895 (like the three-volume novel, which ended in '97 when Heinemann published Hall Caine's *The Christian* in one volume).

Details of dining-room. Seventeenth-century French or Italian drawing above stove. Full of movement. Nymph pursued by satyrs, and Diana sitting with arm extended to hound. (Rather like one of Hester's father's ink-wash sketches.) Circular mirror in heavy gold frame, reflecting the room in miniature.[7] Large silver-framed square mirror in drawing-room, above bookcase all along wall facing window.

After dinner – 10 to 11.30 – we sat with the Hauptmanns in 'the bar'. The H's had guests – a middle-aged German and his wife, both very dignified and respectful – one on each side of G. Hauptmann. (The man was a famous German actor – Kessler? – a 'heavy lead' type.) Frau Hauptmann (who is very short-sighted,

---

[1] Hannen Swaffer, journalist and dramatic critic (1879–1962).

[2] Politician (1863–1937). Knighted 1925. Son of Joe and elder half-brother of Neville.

[3] By Baroness von Tautphoeus (*née* Jemima Montgomery, 1807–93). It was published in three volumes in 1850 and was in its sixth edition by 1863.

[4] Politician and author (1863–1913).

[5] Clement Shorter, journalist and critic (1858–1926).

[6] William Robertson Nicoll, journalist and author (1851–1923). Knighted 1909.

[7] The one which, in Max's unfinished novel *The Mirror of the Past*, reflected the past instead of the present. See *Max Beerbohm and 'The Mirror of the Past'* by Lawrence Danson (Princeton University Library, 1982).

and bathes every day, whatever the weather) was wearing a white silk evening coat buttoned up to the neck – like a nurse in an operating theatre.

I had a P.G. Wodehouse book in my hand – bright red – Hauptmann asked if it was one of my works (*Geschichte*). Frau Hauptmann held it about an inch from her eyes, trying to read the title-page. He then inspected it, while I tried to explain – via Benvenuto as interpreter – what sort of a writer Wodehouse is (no easy task!). In talking or explaining to foreigners, I always find myself speaking in a laboriously correct way, almost as if I were a foreigner who has difficulty in expressing himself in English. How explain Wodehouse to Hauptmanns? 'Is he like Mark Twain?' they ask. It made me realise how entirely untranslatable Wodehouse would be – in German! Then Hauptmann said something, which Frau Hauptmann translated for me as 'I killed the humorist in me long ago'. 'But you have written brilliant comedies,' I replied with unctuous brightness (Max having told me that Hauptmann had written a good comedy, which was performed in London a few times).

I conversed heavily with Frau Hauptmann about myself, and my love of music. She has a very fine Strad, she said, and was a pupil of Joachim.[1] Then we were joined by Lady Mary Rose FitzRoy (a sister of the young Duke of Grafton who was killed while motor-racing last year). She is about eighteen; a pretty little girl who is admired by Benvenuto (three times married and a lady's man). Lady Mary Rose is not at all intelligent, but jolly; cares mainly about hunting. I talked to her about the Grafton and the Pytchley, and hunting in Ireland. She asked me 'Is it your house in Park Lane where they have those lovely exhibitions?' This hunting chatter seemed an absurd contrast to the Hauptmann atmosphere of German culture and the 'great man' business of his celebrity as a writer.

Meanwhile drinks were in circulation – some sort of 'cup' in a huge pewter jug, and red Chianti. I began to talk to Benvenuto about the English translations of his father's works, and offered to influence Faber & Faber about publishing new ones. (A forlorn

---

[1] Joseph Joachim, Hungarian violinist (1831–1907).

hope, I fear.) He spoke bitterly about dear old Ben Huebsch,[1] who published the plays in America, and is, for some reason, anathema with the Hauptmanns.

The whole thing was a bit unreal, owing to my feeling that communication wasn't adequate – a sort of miming-scene compared with one's perfect conversations with Max and Florence. But I felt quite affectionate toward old Hauptmann, who has a charming simplicity about him, in spite of the great man business and his almost artificially 'eminent' appearance. Talking about taking horses over big banks in Tipperary to Lady Mary Rose was, obviously, to be on safer ground than exchanging bows and portentous sentiments with Hauptmann (though he isn't pompous and has much humour in his old face).

There was also a spectacled young German secretary who said nothing. Hester received more of Benvenuto's sentimental and (I suspect) not very accurate anti-Nazi revelations.

13 April (6 p.m.)

Pouring wet day. Have just finished *The Years*, which may be a masterpiece of modern novel-technique but leaves me feeling that I've had a bad overdose of V. Woolf's mind and observations of the world around her. Very inhuman and art-riddled, it seems to me! The poor woman inspects human souls and then throws them away like empty paper bags.

Yesterday was lovely weather and I had a good walk 3-5.30. In the morning we went up to the Hauptmanns' rooms for half-an-hour. He was charming, and showed us his collection of ancient Greek and Roman coins. Frau Hauptmann showed her 1714 Stradivarius – a pale golden one in an old yellow wood case. The violin had a look of great refinement and distinction. There were two canaries in a cage by the high window, and the room was almost too hot with the sunshine which flooded in. '*Kameraden*,' said old Hauptmann, with an urbane wave of the hand at the canaries. He also showed us two tiny carved heads – one (modern?) of Socrates,

---

[1] A charming and humane American publisher of great taste and integrity (1876–1964).

the other ancient Greek or Sicilian, of a woman. Also took us upstairs to see his little work-room with a large roof-balcony – packing-cases of books and disorder, as they leave today.

7.15-10.30 we were at the Villino dining. Max talked about Bernard Shaw and his inability to grow old gracefully. (Reminded me of a detail I'd forgotten – G.B.S. sitting in his high-backed wooden chair at luncheon and running his hands up and down it behind his head.)

I took with me Benvenuto's autograph album, in which he'd asked me to write something (on the only blank page remaining). The book begins in 1910 with Cosima Wagner, and contains Kreisler,[1] d'Albert,[2] Humperdinck,[3] and many other musicians and writers – mostly German. (Old Hauptmann's handwriting is very sensitive and delicate, and so is Kreisler's.) The gem of the book is a superb ink-wash drawing of 'Joseph Conrad in 1907' – with a witty, supposed letter (dated from Elysium 1927) beginning 'Dear Benvenuto Hauptmann' and signed 'Yours shadowily but sincerely Joseph Conrad', in which J.C. implores B.H., via Max as medium, to do well as translator of *Almayer's Folly*. Max had forgotten about this, and the sequel has been ironic and deplorable. B.H. spent eight years muddling idly at that 'Penelope's Web' of a 'free translation'. When finished, he had omitted two whole chapters and had *inserted poems of his own*! To the horror of the Hauptmanns it was 'turned down' by Fischer's, the Berlin publishers. (B.H. has now suggested that he would like to translate *me*!)

The album also contained a preposterously pompous page by W.B. Yeats (1929) which amused and irritated Max very much. (When we got home I took the album into the bar and returned it to its owner, who was alone there with Lady Mary Rose, obviously carrying on a mild flirtation with the poor flattered little girl.) When talking about the old age of G.B.S., Max said 'I believe in extinction'. It isn't seemly to play the mountebank with one foot in the grave, he said.

---

[1] Fritz Kreisler, Austrian violinist and composer (1875–1962).
[2] E.F.C. d'Albert, Anglo-French pianist and composer (1864–1932).
[3] Engelbert Humperdinck, German composer (1854–1921).

Also talked about W.J. Locke,[1] C. Disraeli,[2] G.M. Trevelyan.[3] By 'talked about', I mean that I mentioned them and was well rewarded. Max turns everything one mentions into superb reminiscence and criticism. He also talked about Philip Sassoon's political career. Recalling the 'Ulster Rebellion' luncheon to 250 diehards at 25 Park Lane in 1914, when Bonar Law announced that 'our generous host' had offered to give a Hospital Ship to the 'movement' – awful example of buying political advancement!

14 April (11.45 a.m.)

Weather still cloudy, mild and unsettled. Read a hundred pages of Somerset Maugham's new novel *Theatre* last night; what a relief after the preciosities of V. Woolf! Masterly but merciless is Maugham. His characters are odious and yet likeable. Virginia's are unreal; her novel is a self-conscious 'work of art'.

Both novels come out of pessimistic minds which 'see through' the shams and illusions of life. That is where Max is so comforting. 'I believe in extinction' he said; and I saw him for a moment as a modern Socrates.

His attitude toward life's illusions is courageous but kindly. Virginia lacks gaiety and her satire is shrill and sour. Maugham's satire is bitter and worldly-wise and frustrated. He is sophisticated, without depth of understanding. 'To know all is to despise all,' is his philosophy. 'To know all is to be disappointed in all' seems to be Virginia's. Max knows and *forgives*. He knows that illusions are part of the texture of being alive. *He* has real wisdom, real humanity. He does not scold or complain or sneer or mock or heartlessly dissect. He is fastidious, but his disgust at the crudities and vulgarities of the world is redeemed by humour and stoicism. He accepts and avoids the jungle without blaming it for being what it is. 'In a million years, perhaps, the human race will be civilised,' he remarks, lighting another cigarette. Meanwhile he accepts extinction after death, and continues to be an adorably witty and wise and delightful human being, loving the good things of life

---

[1] Prolific popular novelist (1863–1930).
[2] Coningsby Ralph Disraeli (1867–1936), great-nephew of the statesman.
[3] Historian (1876–1962). O.M. 1930.

47

and illuminating them with his exquisite genius for the urbane and the elegant.

Maugham and V. Woolf do not love life; they seem afraid that it will bite them. At any moment they feel life will develop cancer. Life always ends by being ugly and cruel, they suggest, dreading old age and disbelieving in magnanimity, in their totally different styles. They simply cannot be good-natured about their fellow-creatures. Where Max courteously deplores they distastefully condemn.

18 April (11 a.m.)

G. Hauptmann and his wife left on Tuesday. Benvenuto left on Friday. Weather fine since Wednesday with a cool wind. On Thursday we were at the Villino 4.30-10. (Benvenuto also there.) Last night Max and Florence dined here; as usual it was absolutely delightful. I had spent the afternoon reading J.C. Squire's rather diffuse and undistinguished reminiscences,[1] which made Max's talk seem even better than usual.

20 April (10 p.m.)

On Sunday I walked 11.30-1.30, in grand weather, up above the Genoa road. Hester was headachy and nervy in the afternoon, but well enough to dine at the Villino. (More nerves when we got home.) Yesterday was wet in the afternoon, but cleared up after tea, and we walked up the hill above San Michele. To-day gloriously fine. We lunched at Portofino – langoustes and wild strawberries. Hester in good spirits. After tea I went up to the Villino. Florence had gone to Genoa to see the Ellis Robertses.[2] Max suggested a few improvements to my manuscript. He was wearing his smoking-suit; black-velvet trousers, and buff coat with black-velvet facings and cuffs, and waistcoat to match, delightfully dandified.

I am now feeling so healthy that my brain is much less active than usual. I look ten years younger than I did a fortnight ago.

---

[1] *The Honeysuckle and the Bee* (1937).
[2] R. Ellis Roberts, journalist and author (1879–1953) and his wife Harriet.

22 *April* (*10.30 p.m.*)

Fine weather. Yesterday we were at the Villino 4-6.30. Ellis Roberts and his wife were there. To-day we went to Portofino with Max and Florence for lunch. At 4 we went on to have tea with Colonel Pio at his house above Santa Margherita. The Colonel sang and whistled charmingly to his guitar, while we had tea out of doors. (Mrs Pio, who is English, was ill and couldn't come downstairs.) A heavenly day – the happiest, I think, that we've had since we came here – though all hours spent with Max and Florence are pure enjoyment.

25 *April* (*11.30 p.m.*)

On Friday Hester had a bit of a chill, but we went to tea at the Villino in fine weather. (Drove there in a horse-carriage, and walked home.)

Yesterday was cloudy. Max and Florence came to dinner, and we had a convivial evening, drinking Italian champagne. To-day we went to the Villino at 4 and stayed till 10.30. (6–7 I walked up to San Pantaleone, the little church I am so fond of.) It was an exquisite calm spring evening, and the path along the hill was like Paradise in the yellow sunlight. I thought how I used to walk up there seven years ago, when I was about to return to England – contented because I'd succeeded in finishing Volume Two of *Sherston's Memoirs*, but with no security of happiness – my whole existence, as a feeling human being, dependent on the whims and caprices of Stephen, and three years of spiritual disintegration ahead of me – had I but known it! No need to explain the difference between then and now!

Meanwhile I am unable to go on trying to put on paper the delights of Max's conversation. I just go on absorbing it and luxuriating in it.

29 *April* (*11 p.m.*) *Monday*

Motored up the hill toward Chiavari after tea, and walked with Hester to San Pantaleone and Sant Ambrogio. *Tuesday* we went to Montallegro with Max and Florence for lunch. Weather cool; some rain and hail while we were up there, so we sat indoors 12.45–

49

3.15. *Wednesday* Fine day. 3.15–5 we motored up the valley toward Montallegro, and saw the little theatre among the cypresses. Dined at the Villino. Max much interested about the Duke of Windsor's threatened libel-action against Heinemann's and *Coronation Commentary*.[1] He talked delightfully about the railway hotels he has stayed in (in London); also the Hôtel Buffet de Nord in Paris, with its Louis Philippe atmosphere.

11.30 p.m. O dear, O dear! Our last evening with heavenly Max is over; there will be one more luncheon, and then – I shall not hear his voice until April 1938. I shall not hear that voice which is incomparably the most enjoyable voice alive in my world of living people. Anyway, I've had three weeks and a bit of the 'best company' possible, and I shall patiently wait, eleven months and a bit, to be back again in that oasis of vintage civilisation in this era of plucked eyebrows and bombing aeroplanes destroying beautiful old cities in Spain.

This evening, on the radio, we heard Virginia Woolf – a voice broadcasting badly – a Bloomsbury voice quite out of touch with anything outside of Bloomsbury. Yet Max, who is regarded as being caviare for the general public, was triumphantly successful as a broadcaster last year.

This afternoon Hester and I had a lovely walk up at Montallegro. Perfect weather. The sea on one side and on the other the mountains, their colours and contours made magnificent and satisfying by the vast cloud-shadows. We heard the cuckoo calling – away in the vacancy of the olive-terraced valley – the voice of summer newly come to Italy. And we saw three golden eagles and a buzzard – superb in the liberty of the sky.

Giving me back my manuscript-book, Max said 'Don't be afraid

---

[1] A brilliant essay by Geoffrey Dennis (1892–1963), which Arthur Bryant called 'the truest and best book on the subject of monarchy published in our age'. It was designed to appear at the time of King Edward VIII's coronation, but the abdication intervened and the author wrote two more chapters to cover that momentous event. The book was published in April 1937, a month before the coronation of King George VI. The Duke of Windsor took exception to passages about Mrs Simpson and sued author and publisher for libel. The case was heard on 22 November 1937, and after the defendants had agreed to withdraw the book and remove the offensive passages the charges were withdrawn.

of being too long. Write whatever seems to you amusing and interesting.' And then he began turning out the lights and we went down the steps from the Casetta, and saw a firefly by the front door. The sky was velvet-dark with stars. And then Pasquale, the nice-faced motor-driver, drove us home and our last delightful evening at the Villino was ended.

19 June 1937   *Heytesbury*

My dear Max (and Florence too – when Beerbohm hath perused What'e'er this fond epistolary pen May on this paper put), I am sending you a few scraps of photography, recently culled from periodicals. I wish I could send you Heytesbury House also, so that you could stay in it for a few days (but I fear you would delay returning it, in your inimitably unhastening way, in which case I should be obliged to come and fetch it – though that would be no hardship). How odd the House would look, if dumped down on the site of the Villino; and how odd the Villino would look if it found itself surrounded by our large lawns! Very confusing for George, too.

What I meant to say, before I lapsed into fantasy, was that my loyal attachment to Wiltshire has so far prevented me from going to London. I wrote to Rightenstein – I mean Rothenstein[1] – and he applauded the Exhibition idea in his reply; but nothing has happened since then. Here still I linger, sniffing the syringa, Full ninety miles from town, Phillips & Brown.[2]

Yet, as between you and me, how delightful to loiter on, year after year, discussing the Exhibition, 'Nursing our project with unclouded joy'[3] – two Scholar Gipsies we – shunning those shy traffickers of the Leicester Galleries who in the New Burlington Galleries would fain undo their corded bales—

---

[1] Will Rothenstein, artist and writer (1872–1945), had from 1920 to 1935 been Principal of the Royal College of Art. S.S.'s idea was for a retrospective exhibition of Max's caricatures.
[2] Proprietors of the Leicester Galleries, where Max's exhibitions were shown.
[3] Matthew Arnold, 'The Scholar-Gipsy'.

Max on the Terrace

But no; postpone we still the desired event
While 1940 comes and gently goes,
And the rich colourings of our first infant
Fade to a delicate memorial rose.

O were they dreams – those oft discussed cartoons,
Or do they still at Christie's get snapped up?
And that far-off suggestion of Sassoon's –
That promise that with Rothenstein he'd sup –
Will it take twice ten twelve months to mature,
And be itself a theme for caricature?

No; it shall *not*.
       I'll be like Mussolini; get things done.
       And Rothenstein shall end what I begun.
       I love to think how, at the Private View,
       Cruising around with dull but shrewd regard,
       Old Major Paget, breathing rather hard,
       Remarks, 'A thing we Pagets never do
       Is to lampoon',   Yours truly   S. SASSOON

P.S. I fear this letter contains very little news.
P.P.S. Hester sends her love.
P.P.P.S. The chandeliers send dulcet twinklings.

The photograph makes George's eyes look darker than they are.

18 August 1937   *Hotel Bristol, Villars, Switzerland*

My dear Siegfried,[1] August 17 I breakfasted, dined, supped, and laid at the Bristol Inn. Florence breakfasted, dined, supped and laid at the Bristol Inn. There is here one Major George Paget, a sour stern man, but we find him very agreeable however. He was in the Army. He asked me if I was a Wiccamist. I said I was an

---

[1] *The Diary of a Country Parson* by the Rev. James Woodforde (1740–1803) was discovered and edited by John Baldwyn Beresford (1888–1940) and first published in five volumes between 1924 and 1931. S.S. had sent the first two volumes to Max, who replied in the style of the good parson.

old Chartrousian. He is not a Wiccamist so we have had but little talk together of Winchester. We like him very well. He dined with us at 3 this Aft'noon. The first course was a grand fat Pyke fryed in Honey, a rosted Haunch of Venyzon with Apple Sauce and Oyster Hash over it, 3 young capons boiled in the Swiss fashion, 2 Gooseberry Tarts, and a mash of Turnips. The second course was a round of Cold Beef, Syllabubs, 8 Pig Chops, a Plumb Cake, some Venyzon Pasties, and Veal Soup. We had a Desert of Fruit after Dinner. Oranges, Wallnuts, a Pine Apple, and Apples. There was drank 3 bottles of Omontado, afterwards Beer, Rum and Cyder. We sat long, then went to the Theatre. We had the Front Box, for which I payed o.1.6. The Play was Irène, a translation of Dr Johnson's Irene, the Entertainment was Florodora. The play was well enough, but the Entertainment not becoming, I wishing it were otherwise. The Major liked the Entertainment well, but not the Play, he having not read it in English, I think. For Supper we had a Dish of Mackarel, a Fruit Pie of Bilberries and Cherries, a great handsome Dutch Cheese, broiled Giblets, a Lobster, tosted Cream Cheese, and Peppered Spinnadge with Mush Rooms. There was drank 2 bottles of Port Wine, 1 of Claret, and 2 bowls of Cold Milk Punch. I then played at Picquett with the Major. I won from him o.o.3½, but he did not pay me. I will remind him of it if he do not, but think he will. Going to bed I was seized with some spasms of the stomack and hiccupping which I think was caused by the high Mountain Air here. There is snow on the crests of some of the Mountains here in despite of it being August.

O Lord God Almighty, I do beseech Thee to send here more holesome Weather.

August 18 I breakfasted, dined, supped, and laid at the Bristol Inn. Florence breakfasted, dined, supped, and laid at the Bristol Inn. The Major breakfasted, dined, supped, and laid at the Bristol Inn. I felt poorly in my health when dressing and shaving. The Major seemed strong and well in his health. He payed me o.o.3½. I did not tell him I would have reminded him if he had not payed me. He and I played at Fives against the wall of the Lutheran Chapel. I lost to him o.o.1¾. I paid him o.o.1¾. My good horse Joshua that had borne me hither so well from Rapallo with Florence on the pillion has been ill with the staggers. I have dosed him thrice daily with Gin and Onions but this morning he died. I fear I shall not get a better horse than this poor beast, but God's Will be done. We dined at a quarter after 3, the major dined with us. The first course was as prime a haunch of Horseflesh as ever I ate ... but this is enough, dear Siegfried, to show you how steeped I am in Parson Woodforde. Ever so many thanks for sending him to me. Your doing so showed as much insight as kindness. You were, as usual, right: he's the man for me: I'm devoted to him. The relief of being wafted far away out of the accursèd modern bounds of cleverness! – of finding oneself in the company of a quiet, decent, loveable, unpretentious fool, in Arcadia. You may object to the term *fool*. But, after all, isn't he one? He seems never to have an idea, he seems never to have even *seen* anyone or anything: he just takes people and things dimly as a matter of course. He leaves one to see them *for* him. And one leaps to the occasion. One's imagination is hot and active. One is *there*, on the spot, in Arcadia, all the time. When he does – as all too rarely he does – describe somebody, one is rather mystified. But even so, one hugs the mystery. How about Miss Anne Thomas (May 30, 1786)? What manner of girl was she? The eldest daughter of the Thomases 'is very reserved and not handsome – Miss Betty is very agreeable and pretty – Miss Anne very still and coarse'. To my dying day I shall wonder about Miss Anne. The undescribed multitudes of gentle and simple who figure in the Parson's pages are clear to me: I see them living their Arcadian lives and going their Arcadian ways quietly, rather clumsily, day after day. But Miss Anne? She is my favourite.

The book is a fountain of delight – I was going to say. But that isn't what I *meant* to say, and I take it back. The book is a tranquil pool of joy, and I love every inch of all the duck-weed on it. What a blessing that on that evening in the Common Room of New College (1763, September 7) when the young James had drunk too much and (says he) 'I fell down dead, and cut my Occiput,' he didn't *really* die! For what should we have done without his Diary? We shouldn't have known of what might have been; but I think we should have felt some sort of great vague blank.

I wonder what J.W. would have thought if he had known that

55

he would be delighting us in 1937? He would have opened his large, expressionless eyes very wide indeed, I imagine. His Editor (what a capital Editor and charming person, by the way!) is rather amused that J.W. was reading *Evelina*[1] four years after publication – and finding it 'very clever and sensible'. How much odder that we should be glorying in the not very clever (but in his 'foolish' way very sensible) J.W. after a so much greater lapse of time!

Thanks also for the delightful cuttings from the Press of this our day. Florence and I laughed consumedly over them.

We have been staying here for a whole month or so, but we return tomorrow to the Villino. We wish you were there to greet us. We always think and talk of you so much – *and* of dear little George – the Hesterine and Siegfriedian pet and wonder, whom we long to see.

Our love to all three of you.   Your affectionate MAX

I wonder how far you have got with the new book? So far as I saw it, I'm sure it really is your *best of all*; and I predict that it will continue to be so. Happy author!

21 August 1937   *Heytesbury*

My dear Max, The only adequate reply to your enchanting pages has already been enunciated – i.e. I have asked Sotheran's to send you the final three volumes of Woodforde. Like you, I would enjoy *fifty* volumes; but we must render thanks to Almighty God that there are, at any rate, *five*.

I was certain that J.W. would become your inseparable crony, but I artfully kept back the three later volumes, knowing that they would be a godsend. (I am keeping Vols 4 and 5 unread myself until next winter – having read the others very slowly – positively dreading the time when there is no more.) (There is also a book called *Mr Du Quesne*,[2] compiled by J. Beresford.) Like you, I became aware of the way in which J.W. makes one see his people

---

[1] By Fanny Burney (1778).
[2] A book of essays (1932).

for oneself. I got something of the same sort from *Moll Flanders*, which contains no visual descriptions at all. But of course, diary-writing is a technique in itself. And, like you, I am 'all for' the duck-weed method. The weather; food; details about expenditure; how one enjoys such things. And how you will love the glories of the Custance dinner-parties, and the gradual revelation of the unpalatableness of Mrs Davy as a visitor. Anyhow, J.W. becomes part of one's mental life; one almost feels that one *was* alive in the eighteenth century. How could one possibly *not* have been there, when it is all so real, so everyday, so intimate, so humdrum-human? (and, as you remark, so blessedly remote from the monkey-tricks of the modern mind).

I haven't been able to go on with my book yet, but am hoping to get back into my detachment in the autumn and again enjoy the tightrope-walking feat of putting the past on paper. But, as usual, I am nervous. I can only pray that the afflatus will return to me and that I shall not return to Italy empty-handed.

Meanwhile I have breakfasted, hunted, tea'd, etc at Heytesbury House since May 2, except for a couple of days with my mother in Kent. (London has not seen me all the summer, and I now get my hair cut in Salisbury.)

Darling little George (who sends two photographs to Florence) has, as you will observe, no need to visit the hair-cutter. His hair is very fair, and might indeed be described as 'down'. He weighs $22\frac{1}{2}$ pounds and measures 31 inches. His energy is prodigious, and he seems to us to be a most adorable character. He now crawls most actively (and is believed to have been *disconsolate* when his daddy went away for two days). His greatest intellectual feat so far is to pull down the electric-light switch and then turn his head to see that the chandelier is ablaze with candles. This Hester regards as a sure sign of *genius*. But she inclines to a belief that George will be a second Beethoven – for he has been heard to sing, and has thumped the piano-keys with enthusiasm. His Nannie, whose ideas are homely, contents herself with describing him as 'a proper little party', and warns us that before we are much older he will tire us out with his 'goings on'. Personally I don't mind how much he 'goes on', as long as he continues to be what he is, the joy and pride of my rural existence.

Three bottles of Château Latour live in the sideboard drawer, and are known as 'Beerbohm's bottles' or 'Max's medicine'. Long may they remain there – or rather – I mean—'Soon may they be consumed by their irrepleviable guest-owner'. Other news (a) I made 41 not out in our match here on August Bank Holiday. (It was 82° in the shade and I was at the wicket eighty minutes, 'pulling the game round' after our last batsman had been 'cheaply dismissed'.) (b) The gardener has destroyed fifty-one wasps' nests in the park lately. (Loud cheers from peaches, pears, nectarines, and plums.) (c) Violet ('Flamingo') Bonham Carter[1] is coming to tea on Tuesday. I intend to assume – *pro tem* – the personality of Major Paget. 'Do you mind *repeating* that remark again – I couldn't quite catch your meaning.' This after one of her *brilliant* epigrams.

With love, dearest Max and Florence, from us both, and affectionate warblings from George.   S.S.

---

12 September 1937   *1 The Offices, Heytesbury Art Agency*

My dear Maximilian, It has just struck me that you ought really to be a Duke (old French). I therefore, with a few strokes of the pen, create you Duc de Beerbohm (Florence's tiara follows by special courier).

But that is by the way and a flourish or fanfare introducing the news that I 'at long last' went to London to-day and held a most successful and delightful conference with the smaller of the two presiding spirits at the Leicester Galleries.

Needless to say, he needed no stimulating with regard to 'Retrospective', which is for me the most enchanting event in a future which contains small promise of enchanting occurrences – and the poor past is vanishing in clouds of demolition dust, as I observed this afternoon when I walked through Berkeley Square and realised, rubbing the dust out of my eyes, that a large portion of it and Brook Street had entirely disappeared, and is at present a huge chasm surrounded by hoardings.

I shall be able to send you detailed information in a few days,

---

[1] Lady Violet Bonham Carter, Liberal politician (1887–1969). Daughter of H.H. Asquith. Created Baroness Asquith of Yarnbury 1964.

when Brown & Phillips have thought out their plans. Meanwhile I can report that I spent a blissful half-hour in the basement looking at some of your works; I enjoyed most 'Rothschilds at Play' and King George and Queen Mary being inspected by the proletariat (these two works having found their way back owing to the deaths of their wise and fortunate purchasers in happier times before Berkeley Square was converted into a second Ypres). Brown told me that Sickert[1] has now assumed the role of a patriarch; walks about with a Wotan-like staff and has grown a long Walt Whitman beard. Anyhow I managed to emerge from the Leicester Galleries without having bought up the whole stock of basement Beerbohms (*oeuvres du Duc de Beerbohm*) but I foresee that if I go there much oftener Heytesbury will become a repository second only to Guedalla House.[2]

Meanwhile, dare I suggest that you employ your 'inimitable' art on a Woodforde series? O that 'twere possible! (I will buy the lot! – for the National Gallery.)

Hester and I motored to Norfolk and saw the church at Weston,[3] and stood on Lenwade Bridge. (The old bridge is still there – undemolished, though superseded by a new one, built in 1927.) Hockering, Mattishall, Ringland – there they were, those magic names – on signposts pointing down shady lanes. And the new Rectory (about 1820) is on the site of the old one, and has an authentic Woodforde feeling and appearance – humdrum and secluded. And it was a mid-afternoon of sleepy sunshine and stillness. One felt that Mr and Mrs Custance and the children were somewhere not far away. Mr Du Quesne had, I think, gone to Norwich to see the marionettes. And I felt that the widow of the Archbishop of Canterbury was spending a few weeks at Mr Townshend's fine place a few miles away. But enough of these time-travellings by thought. Our best love travels to Rapallo. And George gets more delightful every day.   S.S.

---

[1] Walter Richard Sickert, artist (1860–1942).
[2] The writer Philip Guedalla (1889–1944) had a large collection of Max's caricatures. The Leicester Galleries exhibited 164 of them in 1945, and the majority are now in the Ashmolean Museum at Oxford.
[3] Weston Longeville, where Woodforde was Rector from 1776 until his death in 1803.

21 September 1937 LEICESTER GALLERIES [*pasted on*]

~~Dear da Vinci, With regard to your projected 'Last Supp~~

Dear Max, I have received an excellent letter from Oliver Brown which I will send to you when I feel that you are 'up to' the strain of reading typescript discussions about 'difficulties' which can – and shall – be eliminated. I will give you the gist: 'We feel that Max's work should be presented in a more intimate way' (than could be done in a large gallery). 'If it were presented in the Leicester Galleries with, at the most, 200 carefully chosen works, we think it would make an even stronger impression. There are however difficulties in the way of this more limited plan, as it is almost impossible for us to find the whole of our galleries vacant at the same time in the Season of next year. We feel that such an exhibition as this ought to be in the Season, which would not leave too much time for collecting the cartoons from various parts of the world. It might be advisable to postpone it for another year ... Attractive as the idea is, we think that financially it is a most unpromising one. (Groans, and sympathetic cheers.) The majority of the works would have to be loans which must be collected at considerable expense and insured by the organisers of the exhibition. There would be little profit from sales as we are likely to have only a few important ones to offer. As regards any revenue that there would be from admissions it is difficult to make an estimate, but looking up our records we have come to the conclusion that the largest crowds visiting Max Beerbohm exhibitions were due to a few cartoons of a highly topical nature ... It is always difficult to estimate the effect of an exhibition on the masses but, of course, we are certain that the more instructed public would receive the exhibition with enthusiasm.' (Prolonged applause and shouts of *Vive Beerbohm, Incomparable Maximilian*, etc.) ... Silence being restored, Oliver 'asks for more' ... 'All these difficulties that I have mentioned would vanish if Max Beerbohm could be induced to show even a few works. Do you think there is any chance of this?'

S.S. cogitat

All this seems to me to point to the fact that an exhibition will take place in May 1939. And O Max, if you could produce those lovely broadcasts, can't – O can't you delight us all just once again – just, O, a little – with just O, one or two (or half a dozen) fantasy cartoons – utterly untopical? Not that it matters if you don't (I say that in self-defence, lest you feel that I am urging you toward the easel). And now I don't know what else to say – except that my inner self demands that exhibition, though it can never materialise as I dream it; only in Heaven will that exhibition be 'presented' in a way which will satisfy me, for we shall all be young at that exhibition (it will be 'dated' 1900, as regards 'modern developments') and all the nice people will be there, in spite of being dead; and all the nasty ones will be at an exhibition of Surrealist Art at the 'Old Nick' Galleries in some sulphurous underworld. At your exhibition there will be a sprinkling of Royalties – Edward VII will have seen the point and will be explaining to Lily Langtry just how excruciatingly funny your drawings of him are – and the Pre-Raphaelites will be roaring with laughter, and even Christina Rossetti will have got the giggles. (Edward VII to Reuben Sassoon: 'Who is that nun? She appears to be having hysterics.') Even Omar Khayyam will be there – arm-in-arm with Edward FitzGerald – and as for Gosse, he will at last be in the seventh heaven – 'My dear FitzGerald, you really *must* introduce me to your distinguished Persian friend, for whose exquisite quatrains I entertain an admiration which yields to none.' And Algernon[1] will present you with an enormous ode, beginning:

'Beerbohm, born in the world's white morn, whom seas and
    spring-tides cradled in art,
Seer and singer and bounteous bringer, seed and spirit of
    twain-fold truth,
Now beholden in galleries golden, our crowned cartoonist
    ensphered apart,
Blinds with thunder and smites asunder the unapparent
    sublime uncouth.'

---

[1] Swinburne.

But my pen is running away with me – running away to Rapallo on wireless waves of innocent exuberation! Yours very truly

S. SASSOON

Heytesbury

14 October 1937

My dear Florence, Hester and I were discussing our plans for next spring ~~yesterday~~ (the day before yesterday – I don't discuss plans on the 13th!) and we decided that we are not going to Venice after all, so I hasten to let you know, in case you are putting yourself to trouble about us. Let me also hasten to add that Rapallo is the town toward which we shall hasten in the middle of April. I shall, I hope, be working hard at my book all the winter, and I pointed out to Hester that Venice is not a good place to go to when one is feeling tired.

So it will be 'the good old Excelsior' again, and Hester seems to like the idea of a week up at Montallegro if there is a spell of really good weather at the end of April. Personally I want nothing but to get a lot more of my book done and then bring it out for Max to read. I have been struggling for nearly three weeks with Chapter 9, and am at last getting into it again.

I have started fair-copying in your lovely spacious manuscript-book, which somehow gives me confidence, and have already got 1700 words on the paper, and it seems to be up to the standard of the previous 'enchantments'. How lovely it will be when we are all together again. The thought will sustain me through the winter, and make my laborious hours easier. My pen seems to move more slowly than ever this autumn, and I wander up and down the music-room under the vast twinkling chandelier like a lost soul – ever and anon returning to my table to put another spontaneous-looking sentence on paper. Last night I spent three hours writing 150 words, and anyone would think they had been written in five minutes!

George is the dearest little boy – he really is! The most lovely, intelligent, and sensitive little face one could wish to see; and so engagingly boisterous, when he isn't gazing around him with those large poet's eyes of his. He weighs $24\frac{1}{2}$ pounds, and stands on his legs quite a lot. How I wish you could have seen him this afternoon (a mild, serene autumn afternoon which seemed unable to realise that equinoctial gales are getting ready to whirl the leaves off our trees). I was riding out and George was going toward the front gates in his pram, sitting up and looking at everything gravely from under his round hat, tied under the chin with a white ribbon. He looked at me, on my enormous horse, in such a self-possessed amused way, as though aware that *size* isn't everything in this world! A baby can be very dignified, can't it? Poor Hester has a bad cold, and is up in her room, reading Lady Battersea's memoirs[1] and wondering whether the new cook will really be worth £100 a year (so far I doubt it). Lady Horner[2] is coming to tea next Tuesday; and that is about all the news at present. With much love from us   S.S.

26 November 1937   *Heytesbury*

My dear Max, As you aren't an O.M. I have just made you an O.B.G. which is a new Order of mine and means Oasis of the Balm of Gilead, which is what you are to my mind, and if you blench from Oriental blandishments, all I can say is:

> Let all the Major Paget in you rise and say,
> 'Bit *too* polite; but quite good fellow in his way'.

Meanwhile this letter is to let you know that I am progressing with what *you* so flatteringly called 'the enchantment'. I finished Book I about three weeks ago, and have called it *The Old Century*. I added three chapters to the eight which you and Florence read, and they totted up to just over 10,000 words. I have since written two chapters of Book II (7000 words) and am now at Marlborough, in 1902.

---

[1] Constance de Rothschild (1843–1931) married in 1877 Cyril Flower, first and last Lord Battersea. Her *Reminiscences* were published in 1922.
[2] Frances (1860–1940), widow of Sir John Horner, wealthy patron of art and artists (1842–1927). They lived at Mells in Somerset. In her youth she had been painted by Rossetti. Her memoirs *Time Remembered* appeared in 1933.

To my regret I have sent Book I to Faber's so that it can be set up in type. I say 'to my regret' because I wanted you to be the first (after Hester) to read the manuscript of the new chapters. (You see the book is dedicated to someone called Max, and I leave you to guess whether it is you or Lord Beaverbrook.)

But I shall be able to send you some nice page-proofs soon, and you will be able to read me more comfortably like that, and offer, I hope, some of your suggestions when you find me lapsing from clarity or deficient in tact or vocal cadence. I have worked every night for nine weeks – usually from midnight until 5 a.m., and begin to feel that I really am one of the bulldog breed – for it is very tiring and the words seldom flow easily. Hester has supplied me with so many nocturnal boiled eggs, cups of Bovril, and spoonfuls of caviar, that I shall soon be a composite of Hen, Ox, and Sturgeon.

> Let all the Sturgeon in me, all the Ox,
> And all the Hen, cry 'Tush' to ticking clocks

is my motto.   S.S.

21 December 1937   *Heytesbury*

Dear Dedicatee, I am sending you the specimen pages of type which has been chosen for my (and your) book. I wanted it to be the same as the first two volumes of *Sherston's Memoirs*, but my publishers were unable to face the prospect of a book which contained less than 300 pages. 'Difficult to market' was their dictum. So Part I *The Old Century* is being set up 'as per enclosed', and Part II *Educational Experiences*[1] will follow suit when finished. I have now completed 49,000 words, and have another 15,000 to write. I shall then be twenty-one and shall take a rest until I can urge myself into being twenty-two etc.

It will be very gratifying to receive '£1000 advance on 25% after 5000', but the publication of this sensitive writing makes me wish that I weren't so sensitive about it. Like you, I shall not 'know myself' when it is popular. The person who wrote it will be somewhere else – hiding.

---

[1] Later changed to *Seven More Years*.

Anyhow I will send you a set of page-proofs of Part I as soon as I have them. With love from us   S.S.

Just fancy! I am reading *Trilby*[1] – and enjoying it. Such is my idea of mental relaxation. Let us hope that I shan't begin to *write* like du Maurier! If I had the energy I would write you a page or two of my autobiography in the idiom of *Trilby*. But O how preferable to most of the 'Moderns'!

Someone sent me Major Paget's travel article in *The Vegetarian*. Such blissful enjoyment comes seldom to mere mortals like me.

9 January 1938   *Heytesbury*

My dear Max, I am in the middle of a book by Vincent O'Sullivan – *Aspects of Wilde*[2] – If you have not seen it, tell Florence – (with a graceful wave of the hand) to let me know, and it shall be Sotheran'd to you without delay. The last thing but one Sotheran'd to you was Vols 3-5 of the Diary of the only clergyman who really matters. Since then, I think, Hester sent you the 'Welbeck Memoirs',[3] feeling that its photographic reproductions would please you. O'Sullivan was recommended to me by Desmond – in the *Sunday Times*. What a comfort Desmond is!

I am proof-correcting! Have got 19,000 words 'in galleys', and am, as usual, perplexed by my punctuation. I get out of it by saying to myself, 'The book is written for reading aloud, and the vocal cadence supplies the punctuation.' However, in April (would that it were here, and I at the Villino!) I shall stand over you until you have straightened out the erratic commas. (I eschew *colons* – I can't think why – sheer clumsiness, I suppose.)

The awful thing is that I've not written a word of 'the last 15,000' yet, and don't feel able to at present. What a lovely book it would be, I think, if it ended at the 49,000th word. Nothing

---

[1] Novel by George du Maurier (1894).
[2] An excellent book, published in 1936. The author was an Irish-American poet and novelist (1868–1940), who spent most of his life in France.
[3] *Men, Women and Things* by the sixth Duke of Portland (1937).

more is needed. (It ends with my housemaster at Marlborough saying goodbye to me with the words 'Try to be less silly'.)

I would ask George to finish it for me, but he knows only thirty words so far (and *that* is only a vain boast of Hester's). I can't end with 15,000 Bow-wows, Moos, Nannies, Daddies, and Mummies, can I? Faber would be distressed, though the modernists might think it a true and profound climax.

Standing over Max

I have discovered a very good book of *flat* Memoirs for you. *Du Maurier and his Friends* by C. Hoyer Millar (who married du M's eldest daughter). It is a thesaurus of clichés and chestnuts. You will adore it. He is in the Major Paget class as a writer.

With love from   S.S.

24 March 1938   *Rural England*

My dear Max

'This time four weeks', Providence permitting, there will be no need for me to address you through the well-worn medium of my 'Waterman'.
Meanwhile I have just stuck the faces of both brothers[1] on an

---
[1] Kings Edward VIII and George VI.

envelope, hoping that five faces will be enough to satisfy the postal authorities.

Enclosing the page-proofs of Part One of my book, which I have sometimes wished, while working, it had been a shorter one. Anyhow, the final chapter of Part Two will soon be finished; and when the task is completed I shall not be sorry it is.

(This, you will observe, is a new stanza-form, with modernist rhyming.)

I have just been reading – for its literary style – the *Estate Magazine*, and here are two specimens. 'Asparagus-growing in this country has certainly come to stay.' 'Rabbits as pets never lose their hold of the public.' In sending you *The Old Century*, I sincerely hope that it will never lose its hold on you. Five more chapters (21,000 words) are in galley-proofs, and the final chapter (my twenty-first birthday) is in the agonies of being composed.

I must explain, by the way, that the insertion on p.104 was made by request of my mother, who wished me to put in an extra word for Uncle Don, whose achievements have been somewhat belittled by Uncle John's family (a family feud – or something not unlike one).

I think you will enjoy Chapter X, for which I have a special feeling myself, and am inclined to rank it with the Edingthorpe one. In my desperation at being unable to produce enough words to satisfy the publisher's desire for a volume of 'easily marketable' length, I suggested that I should print as an appendix my 1906 volume of privately printed juvenilia. I now feel that this would be a mistake, and am anxious to know whether you agree with me. The poems are quite good for a boy of nineteen, but they have no literary value. If you are uncertain I will bring them to Rapallo for you to look at. But surely they would intrude on the reader's enjoyment? (and the 'general public' wouldn't read them at all!).

I am enclosing a proposal I received from the B.B.C. They offered me twenty guineas for my services, and of course I declined, to converse with Mr Jennings,[1] of whom I know nothing, except that I read a dreadfully pert and sophisticated article by him on

---

[1] Humphrey Jennings (1907–50), documentary film-maker.

the Modern Theatre. Can it be possible that Masefield will partake of the proceedings? Jennings: 'What, Mr Poet Laureate Masefield, do you posit as essential to Poetry?' Masefield: 'Beauty' (pronounced 'Bēoutay').

Well Flax – I mean Morence – George is walking about his nursery now, and making enchanting experiments in lingual exercise. (He has gone far beyond 'Bow-Wow', and Hester isn't at all sure that he didn't once murmur 'Paterfamilias'.) Yesterday he was observed to pick two large daisies which he carried for a while and then 'put them back', carefully placing them in an upright position. This seems to show that he has an ingrained sense of order, and I claim that it comes from *me* – as Hester, bless her, loves to leave everything on the floor (including last night's game of unfinished Patience). I can only say that George is perfectly lovely and quite adorable, and I do not doubt that you will believe me.

Last Thursday I went to London for the first time since my September visit to the Leicester Gals – I mean Galleries. This time I gave the Gals a miss and went to *The Three Sisters* instead.[1] But I *shall* just look in on Brown & Phillips before I leave for Italy, merely to tell them that I am on my way to visit 'that grand old lion Max Beerbohm'. (By the way, I once lunched with Mr Macrae,[2] in 1920, in New York, but have lost touch with him ever since.)

You will observe that I've been reading the preface to your Definitive Edition[3] (and I also read, quite lately, your Note on the Einstein Theory; I have seldom enjoyed anything more; it seemed to me absolutely perfect). So are you. With much love from us all (I am teaching George to lisp the word Beerbohm).   S.S.

[S.S. had temporarily dried up as a diarist, but on 26 July 1938 he noted 'On April 21 we went to Rapallo. Stayed there four weeks – Elysian weeks of seeing Max every day.']

---

[1] By Chekhov, directed by Michel St-Denis at the Queen's Theatre, with Peggy Ashcroft, John Gielgud, Gwen Frangcon-Davies, and Michael Redgrave.

[2] John Macrae, head of the American publishing firm E.P. Dutton & Co. who had so described Max.

[3] A limited edition of Max's collected works in ten volumes (1922–8).

My dear Florence, I have just been culling some Tatleriana for Max, but hasten to assure you that England is still quite sane – Heytesbury is anyhow. George is more adorable every day, and astonishes us all by his quickness in learning words, and using them appropriately. (He is very proud of 'syringa'.) I haven't much news, except that I spent nearly two weeks having laryngitis, and since then have done the *final* correcting of my proofs, which are now, I hope, printer-safe. Dick de la Mare[1] has promised to take trouble over the binding, and is getting Mrs Raverat (née Darwin)[2] to make one of her delicate woodcuts for the title-page. Her sketch seemed very charming – a boy fishing, with just the right meditative feeling about it.

During influenza I spent some delightful hours reading Max's dramatic criticisms,[3] and many a quiet chuckle I had – when not gargling my throat. Visitors have been few. David and Rachel (Cecil)[4] came to tea, and were as delightful as ever, but Desmond is still elusive and his week-end here remains in the mists of Desmondism. The days slip away and we never seem to want to go anywhere. Darling George *is* Hester's occupation (apart from 'coping with the cook', who seems to regard Heytesbury – not unnaturally – as a rest-cure). Cricket-matches punctuate the calendar. On June 11th we defeated the 'Oxford scholars blithe',[5] who consumed much cold salmon and junket in 'the old kitchen', which Hester had decorated with beech-branches. We often talk of our lovely times at Rapallo, and look forward to next spring, and the added delight of seeing Dora[6] again. I really think that the Villino (and of course the Casetta) has given me some of the most perfectly happy and harmonious hours of my life. As the saying

---

[1] 1901–86, elder son of the poet, a director of Faber & Faber Ltd.

[2] Gwen Raverat (1885–1957), author of *Period Piece* (1952).

[3] *Around Theatres*, originally published in 1924 as two volumes of the limited edition of Max's collected works. One-volume edition 1953.

[4] Lord David Cecil (1902–86) and his wife Rachel, daughter of Desmond Mac-Carthy.

[5] Matthew Arnold, 'The Scholar Gipsy', with 'scholars' for 'riders'.

[6] Max's sister.

goes, 'it spoils one for everything else'! How flattered you must feel! I always say to Hester, in my blunt way, that we ought to be jolly well thankful to those 'jolly decent' blokes, the Beerbohms. And she, in dulcet accents, agrees with me. This letter, however, contains very little news. I can only refer you to *The Times* (and the *Tatler*). With much love from us   S.S.

1 December 1938   *Heytesbury*

My dear Max, Was it 92 or 62 Inverness Terrace to *which* I sent the 'dedication copy' of *The Old Century*? I have lost MacColl's[1] letter *which* 'put me wise as to your whereabouts', and am perplexed into addressing this to the Athenaeum, *which* is, however, a very respectable address and ought to find you, as long as they don't send the letter on to Rapallo. The subject about *which* (that's the fourth which, which shows that my prose is deteriorating owing to losing touch with you) I am writing to you is a delicate one. Being temperamentally averse to meeting my best friends in the uproar of the metropolis (and prevented from attending Dora's bazaar, which was a great disappointment) I am wondering whether you and Florence will be able to visit our Trollopian neighbourhood for a cosy week in the country. Whether? Perish the word! *When?* That is the question.

Would Yuletide attract you? (Hester will be waiting for you aneath the mistletoe.) You will find us quiet to the point of stagnation. No guests or festivities – just a few bottles of Mouton-Rothschild etc, and a local turkey which is still conceitedly unconscious that I am going to carve it. And if you find us too quiet, I can send for Rex Whistler and his poet brother,[2] because their parents now live in Salisbury Close, and they will be there for Christmas. Anyhow come whenever you can, dear Max, for I am famished for your society; and George begins to need a glimpse of his stern unbending godparents. (Ought you to hear him his Catechism, I wonder?)

Judging by your *Garland* – what *you* don't know about Christ-

---

[1] D.S. MacColl, painter and art critic (1859–1948).
[2] Rex, artist (1905–44). Laurence, poet and engraver on glass (born 1912).

mas isn't worth knowing.[1] (Ah, ha! But suppose I was to design you a *D.H. Lawrence* Christmas!)

'Plum pudding is a blasphemy against sex-subconsciousness.'

Yours ever   S.S.

16 December 1938   *62 Inverness Terrace, W.2.*[2]

Dearest Siegfried, First of all, let me mention that I've read *The Old Century* twice since publication – and with ever-increasing joy therein. It is a wondrous work; but this I told you in Rap, of course: a miracle of evocation; and its only fault is that it uncharitably cheapens all other work of the kind. I shall always be immensely proud of the dedication, *and* of the manuscript stanzas against the dark blue globe; only wishing I had a real right to such things. Meanwhile, I long to know how the succeeding vol is shaping. Not *easily*, I am sure. But what would life – or rather art – be without difficulties? I like to think of you frowning at your desk, and rising and strolling up and down, and then unknitting your brow, and smiling, and resuming your seat, and going ahead happily.

Florence (whose signature you forged with such success) wrote to you the other day, saying how very, very sorry we were we shouldn't be able to come and spend Christmas with you and Hester – and George. If we might come early in January . . . ? Our friend Dorothy Lanni of Drugolo is due to arrive in London at the end of the old year, for a few days. After which we should be

---

[1] Max's *A Christmas Garland* (1912) contains brilliant parodies of seventeen contemporary writers, all connected with Christmas.

[2] The Beerbohms had returned to England at the time of the Munich crisis.

free for Wilts. But if that sort of date wouldn't suit you well, do please postpone us without a qualm.

We have had rather a sad time lately. My dear niece Viola died, as you know.[1] And since then my oldest friend, Reggie Turner, has died too – the inimitable and golden-hearted Reggie.[2] Such losses aren't borne lightly.

Please let us know about our visit as soon as you know what your plans are. My fond love to you both, and to the dear third party for whose catechism I am so unworthily responsible. MAX

19 December 1938 [*late at night*]   *Heytesbury*

My dear Max, I have just read your letter, which I had 'kept for a treat' since its five o'clock arrival. The high music-room windows are 'frosted glass' (like those table-jugs one used to pour claret-cup out of at parties given by people like Major Horrocks[3] on their lawns), but the cruel bitter frost outside (which is 'putting the kibosh on' the optimism of those nice thrushes of ours who were singing to me and George on Friday as though it were *April* 16) is (for cosy self) counteracted by a glowing, purring log-fire; and Robbie Ross's clock is ticking briskly in its selfish little assurance that I shall continue to wind it up every eight days.

> Now sleeps the Château Margaux, now the Mout-
> On-Rothschild, in hot-water-pipe-warmed vault.[4]

The vintages themselves are unaware of – but bouquet-ishly resigned to – the fact that (we hope) you will lift them to your lips *quite early in 1939* (*vide* invitation from Hester to Florence). A nice dry Carbonnieux is also there (Mr Beerbohm's luncheon wine).

I always say to Hester that bad though the state of Europe may be (and she follows its varying political fomentations with a perusive anxiety which suggests that *she* is personally responsible

---

[1] Viola Tree, actress (1884–1938).
[2] Novelist (1869–1938). Max's dearest friend. See his *Letters to Reggie Turner* (1964).
[3] A neighbour in S.S.'s youth (see *The Old Century*).
[4] cf Tennyson, 'Now sleeps the crimson petal . . . ' in 'The Princess'.

72

for the future of Poland, Roumania, and other extensive regions of which she has, actually, no first-hand knowledge) *there is always Major Paget to put things into their proper perspective* – adding that 'when Max comes to stay, low though the thermometer may stand, the air of Heytesbury House will be filled with sounds and sweet airs that give delight and harm not'.[1] But I am waxing fulsome. (My Persian ancestry included silken wheedlers, I suspect!) O Max, *why do you have* this epistolary effect on me? (That Dora of yours does something similar to me – I become almost foolishly 'forthcoming' – as Henry James would say.)

Recently I re-read 'The Lesson of the Master'.[2] What a lovely piece of writing. In the Pan-Fascist Future I shall read no one except Henry James – and you. (There I am again – you see – just an Oriental court-flatterer!) ... Do you know Algebra? These brackets of mine are reminiscent of him, aren't they? Talking about school-life, I had such a funny letter lately, from an old Bradley (A.G.)[3] who dictated, at the age of eighty-eight, his memories of Mr Gould (of Marlborough). 'I had many of his champagne dinners, at which he got a bit incoherent, but nobody minded, he was a privileged person. He had a fine croquet ground, on which he and I had many *tight matches*. The school bell often rang before we had finished, but it didn't matter – we finished all right, though he muttered something about "his form".'

To turn to sadness (unwillingly) I thought of you when I read Reggie Turner's name in *The Times* (and of your loss in Viola too). I only met R.T. once, at Frankie Schuster's, and he made me feel that he was the best company in the world. How grateful I am to the Reggies of this world, who simply refuse to be boring!

People come here to tea and talk doggedly about air-raids and infantile paralysis (as though such things were 'news to me'!). On such occasions I feel inclined to quote Pater at them – to remind them of the splendour of their experience and its awful brevity, gathering all they are into one desperate effort to see and touch. But it wouldn't do. On my porticoed doorstep, unobservant even

---

[1] Shakespeare, *The Tempest*, Act III Scene 2, with 'harm' for 'hurt'.
[2] A short story in Henry James's volume of that name (1892).
[3] Arthur Granville Bradley, author (1850–1943).

73

of the evening star, they would 'tap their foreheads significantly' –
and continue to discuss air-raids and infantile paralysis in the car
on the way home . . . By the way, Max, 'The women that I picked
spoke sweet and low And yet they gave tongue. "Hound Voices"
were they all.'[1] (From a recently printed poem by Willie Yeats.)
With love from   S.S.

Solemn news. I have done *no* writing this winter. The crisis 'did
me in'. I need *you* to launch me on another volume (dedicated 'To
my friend Bax Meerbohm', with apologies for having a cold in the
head).

29 December 1938   *62 Inverness Terrace, W.2*

Dearest Siegfried, This can't be anything at all in the way of
answer to your fascinating letter. Nor shall I be able to answer it
worthily by word of mouth when I see you. I rejoice to think that
Hester and you *can* not inconveniently let us come on Saturday –
and that within forty-eight hours we shall actually be in that
beautiful house with its beautiful inmates. I have ventured to ask
old George Paget to come with us – and have received a rather
curt acceptance: his manners leave much to be desired, and I'm
not at all sure that his heart is in the right place; but you are so
charitable and understanding, and you'll like him. He can sleep on
the stairs, and use our bathroom.   Your affectionate   MAX

Siegfried's 1939 Diary

1 January 1939 midnight

The comfortable texture of prosperous mental life can't be
reproduced on paper; one might as well try to chronicle the
sensations produced by a good bottle of wine, consumed in the
pluperfect company of Max (who arrived here with Florence at
5.45 yesterday). The dry Carbonnieux we drank at luncheon

---

[1] 'Hound Voice', published in the *London Mercury* December 1938. Included in
Yeats's *Last Poems and Plays* (1940).

today fitted well with the cheerful winter sunshine which flooded our dining-room (clear golden wine with a bracing flavour to it). The Château Margaux we drank at dinner had a rich floral bouquet which suited Max's vintage conversation ... But I am writing too elaborately. Better to say that he is a dear and that he never fails to be amusing and genially philosophical, with his enchanting convention of beautiful manners, his exquisitely spontaneous artificiality, his wit which is always funny, and his fun which is always witty.

Anyhow (having refilled my pen with red ink, just to show that this is a red-letter day) we lunched and dined delightfully, and Laurence Whistler brought Jill Furse to tea – charming, gifted and good-looking young people to the highest degree of attractiveness.[1]

2 January (after midnight)

Meals, with Max here, are long and leisurely (except when I am carving turkey and ham and pheasant and hopping about as anxious host – Hester an equally anxious hostess though less 'on her legs').

Talking about Hardy after dinner, Max said that he was always completely natural in his manners when he used to come to the Savile Club and sit at the '*Saturday Review* table' with Gosse and others. 'Meredith's modesty took the form of giving a brilliant performance, as though his fame were not enough and further efforts were required of him. Hardy's modesty was the unassuming sort. And when being entertained at grand houses he made no attempt to "shine". He (as Gosse said) expected the brilliantly bediamonded dowagers to *amuse him*.'

But I know Max too well now to feel any inclination to record his conversation. I just delight in it, and delight just as much in the fact that he is enjoying his visit to Heytesbury and can feel entirely at his ease in our company.

Sunday 8 January (11.30 p.m.)

Max and Florence returned to London this afternoon (leaving the house at 5). Their visit was shortened by three days owing to

---

[1] For their happy marriage and its tragic end, see *The Initials in the Heart* by Laurence Whistler (1964).

the death, last night, of Max's sister Constance (aged eighty-three) who has been failing, so it wasn't unexpected. (Poor Max has also lost Viola Tree, Reggie Turner, and Mrs Pio in the last three months.) My depression at his departure is mitigated by my hope that we shall see him here again in April (which will make up for our not being able to go to Rapallo this year even if he were there). And we have had a perfect week of his society.

27 January 1939   *Heytesbury*

My dear Max, To revert to the Benson Medal,[1] a mild maelstrom has been agitating the metaphoric pool of academic stagnancy which it occupies. As you may have been informed, our Ruth[2] has been elevated to our Olympus and has ceased to be eligible. Sturge Moore[3] has put forward a candidate whose claims to medaldom are, in my 'umble opinion, non-existent. And now Eddie Marsh[4] is urging everyone to vote for Christopher Hassall, who is, as you have heard, a very gifted young poet.[5] I have voted for him: and E.M. has asked me to solicit your support. He has already 'collected' Maurice Baring[6] and Hugh Walpole,[7] and has lively hopes of Binyon[8] and Dunsany.[9] I am hoping that success will crown E.M.'s efforts, thereby saving him from the blues, the dumps, the doldrums and the jitters.

Since you were here I've read several more Henry James stories, and am becoming deeply addicted to his enchantments. He seems to be an ideal antidote to 1939 and its noises. Not that there *have* been

---

[1] The A.C. Benson medal presented occasionally by the Royal Society of Literature.
[2] Ruth Pitter, poet (born 1897).
[3] Poet (1870–1944).
[4] Edward Marsh (1872–1953), civil servant, translator, patron of poets and painters. Knighted 1937. See *The Weald of Youth*.
[5] Poet, playwright and biographer (1912–63). He was awarded the Benson Medal in 1939 and also the Hawthornden Prize.
[6] Poet, novelist, diplomat and man of letters (1874–1946).
[7] Novelist (1884–1941).
[8] Laurence Binyon, poet and art critic (1869–1943).
[9] Lord Dunsany, Irish novelist and playwright (1878–1957).

many here, except in the papers. Weight of snowfall has broken a limb off both our cedars; but no one will notice the difference.

I have been invited to attend a World Congress of the Pen Club in New York on May 8th.

> Shall I be there? O boy, don't you believe it!
> Let's have our Congress here – and never leave it!

With love to Florence and hoping that you are now snug in Surrey near kind Mr Schiff.[1]   S.S.

23 March 1939   *Heytesbury*

My dear Max, I am sending you the lecture which elicited so many groans from me while I was composing it – though I must add that it was loudly applauded by a large audience, many of whom had overheard it only in patches, owing to the perfidious acoustics of the sumptuous hall in which it was delivered.[2] Rather a good version of 'the face' on the title-page (I cribbed the eyes from your caricature!).

Well, I haven't much news – except purely local news – for I haven't been away since you were here, and news-carriers from the outside world have been few – though, after all, why should you *want* to hear any 'news', except that George and Hester are flourishing, and the buttercups in the park a sheet of gold (caused by the grass being cut very late last year, I am told). Would that you were even now burnishing your boots among them!

We are hoping to hear from Florence that you will be wending your ways to Wiltshire when the weather is welcomingly warm. Why not a week in mid-July? or any time after July 4. Eddie Marsh and the poet Hassall are due here that week-end. With much love from us all.   S.S.

---

[1] Sydney Schiff (died 1944) wrote novels as Stephen Hudson. He and his wife Violet lent the Beerbohms a cottage on their land at Abinger in Surrey. They moved there in February 1939 and lived there happily until they were bombed out in August 1944. Thereafter they stayed with other friends until they returned to Rapallo in 1947.

[2] *On Poetry*, delivered by S.S. in the University of Bristol on 16 March 1939 and published as a pamphlet on 18 May.

ON POETRY

SIEGFRIED SASSOON

Arthur Skemp
Memorial Lecturer
1939

" That Face again :"

Printed for the
UNIVERSITY OF BRISTOL
by J. W. ARROWSMITH LTD., 12 SMALL STREET

Dearest Sir Max, (My favourite Knight),[1] Here is a little book for you.

I am pottering along, playing in cricket-matches for Heytesbury and talking about the weather (which leaves something to be desired, except that it has kept everything beautifully green).

I haven't been to London since that day when you were here, and feel rather like part of the landscape. How odd if I woke up and found myself a haystack! – or, worse still, a wasp. (Perish the thought!) But perhaps it will only be 'a J.P.' after all. You, anyhow, are always an Oasis (in this decivilizing age). Sir Oasis and Lady Beerbohm. With which compliment, and lively hopes of seeing you again, and much love from us all. S.S.

When everything but Chaos cracks.
And Peace retires to some sweet far land,
I too retreat – to be with Max –
And read once more *A Christmas Garland*.

S.S.

My dear Max, Chancing to be at Christie's a few days ago, while the Fudge Collection was 'up', I was able to secure an interesting little portrait study which possesses just the enigmatic element that has always appealed to connoisseurs of a (perhaps elusive) category in which you and I can – one hopes – claim to be included. (As usual, I am all at sea with my 'thats' and 'whiches'!) Needless to say, I 'caught the auctioneer's eye' at the earliest possible moment, and after a brisk bout of bidding with Brown (& Phillips) I was happy to secure the little gem for a modest 'monkey'. There was

---

[1] Max had received his knighthood in June 1939.

quite a little cluster of art-critics around me while I was preparing to carry away my prize! Marriott[1] 'gave it' to Modigliani. Borenius[2] and Berenson[3] rather sat on the fence, suggesting that it might be an interesting anticipation of modernist technique by Osberto di Montegufoni,[4] or, possibly, Ruggero Fryi[5] (in his middle manner). Personally, I plump for Ben Nicholson (in his neo-classical period). There is 'something' about the 'treatment' of the upper part of the face, I admit, which reminds me of Maxwell[6] di Villino Chiaro, but *look at the linear 'arrangement' of the mouth and chin.* Anyhow I give it to you; and I hope that you will regard it as a final liquidation of the monkey which you so kindly loaned me after that unlucky Epsom of mine a year or two ago, when I put my shirt on that wretched animal of dear old 'Pug' Pontefract's!

Yours ever   S.S.

Naturally enough, I have instructed the porter at the Athenaeum to forward the picture to your Surrey address, which is – alas – unknown to me!

1 November 1939 *Heytesbury*

My dear Max, Since I am unable to talk to you, I must 'jolly well' write to you, for I have news from (Prose) Parnassus which particularly concerns you, as 'punctuation's Pioneer' ... Well, Maxwell (exquisite prosaist – not better known bootmaker with & Co added)[7] I have 'at long last' made another beginning, and Volume Two is now seven days old (and not yet christened).[8] It was the War that did it, I think. The newspapers just drove me

---

[1] Charles Marriott (1869–1957). Novelist, and art critic of *The Times* (1924–40).

[2] Tancred Borenius, Finnish art-historian (1885–1948).

[3] Bernhard Berenson, art-critic (1865–1959).

[4] Osbert Sitwell.

[5] Roger Fry, painter and art-critic (1866–1934).

[6] S.S. knew that Max's name was Maximilian, but he must have discovered that Max's early set of 'Club Types' caricatures appeared, for some unknown reason, in the *Strand Magazine* (1892) as by H. Maxwell Beerbohm. This letter probably refers to one of S.S.'s caricatures.

[7] Maxwell & Co., famous London bootmakers.

[8] *The Weald of Youth* (published on 15 October, 1942).

away from *1939*; and how happy I've been during my six days' revisitation of *1909*! Sternly forbidding Hester to eat so much as an omelette at the same table with me, eschewing the society of even George (except on his third birthday, when I took tea with him) and passing the *Daily Expresses* and *Telegraphs* on Hester's table in the green drawing-room as though they would bite me if I came within headline's reach of them – by exercising these and other precautions I have 'done' 3200 words of pencil-draft of Chapter I (dear old Chap!) and am this evening resting on my supposititious laurels. What else remains but to write and tell you that I have resumed operations on the delectable treadmill of nostalgic reminiscence? ('*Prosaiste malgré lui*' – as Enoch Soames would say.)

Will you, once more, 'tread the sweet path' of proof-correcting with me? – distant though that day will, I fear, be.

For I have you in mind while I am writing, and I remember your advice – two-and-a-half years ago – 'don't be afraid of being too long; write freely of whatever interests you'.

The delight of being back again in that other world of transmuted memory is like coming to life again after – not being very much alive! About a year ago you harrowed my stagnation by visualising me – in a charming letter – as walking up and down the room and then writing something down and smiling at what I'd done. That is exactly what I was doing last night (and what I ought to be doing to-night if my brain hadn't begged for a holiday, in which to write to you).

No reply is needed. (Your invisible good wishes are enough.) Think of me plugging on and imbibing Valentine's best Juice when my energies are fading out of me.[1]

Meanwhile Heytesbury is much the same as usual, except for the 'evacuees' in the back regions. There have been as many as twenty of them, but they trickle back to town at times, and at present their numbers are, mercifully, reduced to about fifteen – mostly children. Hester is concerned about their future; but I callously remind her that they will make an utter mess of it,

---

[1] Valentine's Meat Juice, manufactured at Richmond, Virginia, was popular here in the early years of this century.

however hard she tries to counteract the edicts of Providence. Anyhow it is nice to think that they are staying with us for a bit and getting some country air; and it will be nicer still when the cause of their coming is concluded. Nicest of all when the clarets and burgundies are in circulation again, and Florence is helping Hester make the coffee, while you and I discuss the high birds we brought down in Heytesbury Wood that afternoon, and the dear old days when we used to hunt with Willie Yeats's Hounds in Sligo. S.S. '*What* a one he was to go!' M.B. 'Never saw a man to beat him when hounds were screaming along on a breast-high scent! Even George Moore couldn't hold his own with Willie – however well-mounted he was.' S.S. 'Was not Lady Gregory a fairly hard woman to hounds?' M.B. 'No, Sir. Lady Gregory, whatsoever else she may have been, was psychologically incapable of ever seeing the end of a "quick thing in the open". But old Willie would have seen his fox pulled down and eaten if you'd put him on a Tipperary ass. "Arrah" – as he used to say ... Yes; first a little more maraschino, thank you ...' Nonsensical as ever, you see! And why *must* I always be *harping* on poor old Butler Yeats? He never did *me* any harm. It's all *your* fault, Max! It was you that started pulling his leg; and, as usual, I never know when to stop (*vide* the Sitwell caricatures). With love to Florence and from us all   S.S.

29 November 1939   *Heytesbury*

My dear Max, I must send you just a few lines (*are* you the night porter at the Athenaeum, by the way? I have just visualised you as sitting there receiving my envelope from the postman – sitting, I would prefer, in one of those leather chair-tents which once lent character to the front-halls of great houses in St James's Square of hallowed memory). What bright fires used to burn in those halls – the clock ticking slowly – 'Her ladyship not back yet from Bridgewater 'Ouse?' – queries the under-steward. ' "*Back yet?*" She'll be dancing 'er 'eels off till the milk comes 'ome,' mumbles the night-porter. *Thackeray* was the man for that sort of thing, wasn't he, Max?

Well, I've pencil-written 18,300 words of *The Weald of Youth* –

my new book of nostalgic and breezy reminiscences of 1908–14. And I'm pleased with it, so far. There are passages in it which will, as I hope for Heaven, console you momentarily for the age we exist in. Too tired to continue, I am now transcribing. And when Hester has type-written, and Faber's have galley-proofed, you, and none other, shall have a look at it. Here is my first sentence – in case it isn't *quite* the beginning you need.

Late one afternoon, at the end of May in the year 1909, I was driving myself home from Tunbridge Wells in the new dog-cart, which was a very comfortable one, two-wheeled, rubber-tyred, and much the same colour as a glass of brown sherry.   With love from us all to you and Florence.   S.S.

O Max, this world is *awful*! But it has always been the same. Civilisation hanging on by the skin of its teeth. And *will* be the same in a thousand years. '*Just* the same. He must remember that,' as H.G. Wells might say, pausing on his walking-tour to Utopia. '*Why not fly?*' he adds, in an hallucinatory afterthought. And does so – 'crashing' (the inverted commas are dear old Henry James's) in the next field but one.

[*28 May 1940*]   *Charing Cross Hotel, London, W.C.2*

My dearest Siegfried, How long it is since I have owed you a letter! I am indeed the worst of bad correspondents – and you are the best: I mean you write such splendid letters – with poems and drawings to match. I do hope you and Hester and George are well and – no, *happy* I can't hope, except in the case of George, so black is our present world, and so obscure the future (though I firmly believe that the defeat of the Germans is in that future, right enough, in spite of all). Florence and I have been here for a week, for a sad reason. Darling Dora fell down a flight of stairs at the Priory, and broke her arm. She was taken at once to the London Hospital. She does not seem to have had any internal injuries; but of course she has always been delicate, and is now old, and it is hardly to be expected now that she can survive. Her mind is perfectly clear, and she talks exactly in her own delightful way. She does not at all wish to die. She feels that she has had a very happy life, and she has of course a firm belief in life to come. Yesterday she spoke of you and Hester with great affection. Your letters had pleased and moved her so much. You might perhaps send her a few words of sympathy – though perhaps she might not live to read them ... We don't let her know exactly how the war is going: the accounts we give her are rather garbled; for we don't want her to think that all is not fairly well. The doctors and nurses of course do not let her suffer much: she is given frequent sedatives. Her voice is weak, but, like her mind, perfectly clear – and happy, like her face.

Dearest Siegfried and Hester, we know how sorry you will be. We send you our fondest love. Your affectionate   MAX

29 May [*1940*]   *Heytesbury*

My dearest Max, Dora has seemed very much like a Saint, to me, and has her reward in serenity of spirit, I know. It is for *you* that my eyes are full of tears. But I insist on 'smiling through them' at you. A sorrow's crown of sorrows is *not* having any happier things to remember, isn't it?[1] And you have lovely things to remember, haven't you?

I don't want to be pompous and 'leading article-ish'; but I know your passionate loyalty to England and its finest elements; and I try to believe that in these bad times all our best people *are* England. We are all either John Bull or Britannia – according to our temperaments! Like you, I firmly believe that the Abomination of Desolation will be defeated, though the 'news' has been rather difficult to stand up to lately.

Meanwhile I continue to read Henry James (his middle-period shorter works), he being 'so all beautifully remote' from Hitlerism and its brutal behaviour. I can't do anything else, except go for a ride and play with George and counteract, by rather forced cheerfulness, Hester's not unnatural anxiety about Armageddon.

---

[1] 'This is truth the poet sings, That a sorrow's crown of sorrow is remembering happier things.' (Tennyson, 'Locksley Hall'.)

The *Observer* is printing a little poem of mine next Sunday. I hope I haven't overdone the 'grand style' note, and that it may hearten a few people – shattered with anxiety and strain as they must be. With much love to you and Florence from us all   S.S.

The English Spirit

Apollyon having decided to employ
His anger of blind armaments for this –
That every valued virtue and guarded joy
Might grieve bewildered by a bombed abyss –
    The ghosts of those who have wrought our English Past
    Stand near us now in unimpassioned ranks
    Till we have braved and broken and overcast
    The cultural crusade of Teuton tanks.[1]

10 October 1940   *Heytesbury*

Dearest Max, Many a time I have written you an unwritten letter – during the unspeakableness of the 'late lamented' months; and often I have wanted to hear news of Dora.[2] But one's finer faculties seem to have been dazed; and writing to you doesn't belong to anything except delightfulness of mind; I can't associate communication with you with bombs and black-outs and belovèd Britain beset by barbarians!

Even now my pen can't easily be controlled from frisking off into a spate of sprightliness to the music of entrancing memories – in that ballroom where our minds have waltzed together so serenely. So even now – 'Can I have the second "supper-extra"?'

O Maxwell, who in dear dead days
Made life, for me, one mayonnaise –
One sole-supreme of heavenly talk –
O Maxwell (*sings*) 'Where'er you walk!'

---

[1] Written on 19 May 1940, published in the *Observer* 26 May, and in *Rhymed Ruminations* (1942).

[2] Max's sister Dora, who had been a nun for most of her life, died on 13 August 1940.

This evening I've been reading some charming letters from Thackeray to his daughters (did you ever meet old Lady Ritchie?) and three hours melted away as easily as a strawberry ice. I was safe in the past – away from this detestable interregnum between a wrecked civilisation and the bleary dawn of (let us hope) a new one.

However, we must try and plume ourselves upon being such heroes – standing to attention while Winston (for whom cheers three-times-three, I think you will agree) exhorts us – between explosions (*vide* his perorations, *passim*).

> But, oh dear, oh dear, oh dear, oh dear,
> I wish that this were now next year;
> Or, better still, that me and you
> Were pledging Peace in '42!

A few weeks ago I was asked to write an article for the *Fortnightly* (which I had believed to be defunct); so to pass the time I composed a chatty sort of essay on 'Aliveness in Literature'. Not a very well-written or closely reasoned article, I fear. I mention this because I took the liberty of referring to your prose writings – clumsy lout that I am! So look out for it in November. (No one else will!)[1]

Some fine day in the far future, I am hoping, I shall be elected editor of our parish magazine. I shall invite you to contribute a sonnet (it must be on some subject connected with agriculture or the future life, or the vicar may blue-pencil it out). Meanwhile, things aren't outwardly altered much here. A large camp is being built in a field outside our woods, but one isn't aware of it unless one goes and looks. We have fifteen refugee children and a matron in the back regions, but their merry shouts rather cheer one up. (The families who were here last winter made the place into a slum and took advantage of Hester's good-nature to an extreme degree. They left in May; lousy and ungrateful!) We have been threatened – recurrently – with many more visitors – billeting of troops and lord knows what else – but the danger seems to have passed, and I am still in undisputed occupation of my upstairs room and its

---

[1] It appeared in the November 1940 number of the *Fortnightly Review*.

bookcase full of association copies. George has taken to pro-
nouncing his e's and i's as o's − i.e. 'Gov moy Mox Gohrbome's
Ossoys'. His height is now 3ft.6in. He *is*, and promises to be, one
of the most delightful people imaginable. All the gardeners are
now under his spell; they neglect their bedding-out and pruning,
and prance like lambkins to his piping. I haven't had a meal
away from here since early in April, when I went to town for one
night's revelry with the Byam Shaws. (He is now a captain in
the Royal Scots.)[1] But Heytesbury is always lovely to look upon
and I don't really mind the monotony. With much love from
us all   S.S.

Dearest Florence, Do send us a post-card, please.

Your old admirer   S.S.

4 July 1941   *Heytesbury*

My dear Max, I am sending you a scrap of prose from my still
unfinished continuation of *The Old Century* (Geoffrey Keynes[2]
had some eighteenth-century paper which he wanted to use, so I
gave him this Royal Academy picture in the old style).[3] I worked
very hard at my book for three months in February, March, and
April, but have still got two more chapters to write and have fallen
into a state of lawn-weeding idleness which bids fair to cause my
publisher to send me frantic telegrams imploring me to 'send copy
soon as possible'. Anyhow I will send you some page-proofs in a
few weeks, but in these harassing times I feel unwilling to ask you
to put yourself to trouble marking them; it will be enough if I can
feel that my chapters have given you a little pleasure and escape
from − we all know what!

This morning I received a postcard from Will Rothenstein, who

[1] Glen Byam Shaw, actor and theatrical director (1904−86), and his actress wife
Angela Baddeley (1904−76).
[2] Surgeon, book-collector and bibliographer (1887−1982). He arranged the publication of several of S.S.'s later limited editions, and published his bibliography
of S.S.'s works in 1962.
[3] *Early Morning Long Ago*, privately printed in an edition of fifty copies in March
1941.

is coming to these parts to lecture to the soldiers, so I am hoping that he will stay a night here, which will be a great treat, as we see so few people and so seldom get a nice talk about 'things that matter'.

My writing-room is now hung with exquisite pictures by Boudin, Fantin-Latour, Renoir, Forain, and other French masters, and there are good pictures all over the house, leaning against walls, tucked away in wardrobes, and suspended in unfrequented bedrooms. My lawyer, J.G. Lousada, sent his collection here — about a hundred oil-paintings and water-colours. I wish you could see them – but I am always wishing that you were here.

I haven't been away at all for fifteen months. You will smile when I tell you that the only time I nearly went away was quite lately, when I was invited by Blunden to Merton College to address the Max Beerbohm Society!

I was going – and gladly – to ladle out some of my Oriental fulsomeness about your prose writings, but a violent attack of lumbago prevented me. So you weren't adulated after all.

A terrible book has been published lately about the Sassoon Family – terrible in its journalese and very superficial and gossip-columnish in its contents.[1] But there is enough in it to interest you a little. It gave me one fact I didn't know – i.e. that one of my great-uncles married his great-niece!

I am sending Florence a photograph of George, taken four months ago, and I hope that this will persuade her to send us a letter with some news of you both. This is rather a flat letter – lumbago has affected my exuberance of mind. With much love, dearest Max, from   S.S.

George *is* a dear, isn't he? He rushes about at top-speed, talks in a loud voice, and is the joy of my life.

26 January 1942   *Heytesbury*

My dear Max, If you haven't been inundated with letters – congratulating and thanking you on and for your spoken essay – but

---

[1] *The Sassoon Dynasty* by Cecil Roth (1941).

I am sure you *have*![1] That is why I have waited a few days. I have owed you a letter for a long time, and now owe you a double one, since you wrote us all – everywhere – the most delightful letter possible, on that infernally foggy Sunday evening – which made me shudder to think of you being obliged to go to London in such weather. You 'told us tales of giants' and did it 'in the dell'. We gathered round in our multitudes – 'O do listen to dear Sir Max ... he's *singing* ... '*Don't push* me like that!' 'Be quiet, Margot; no one told *you* to say anything'. 'Have a bit of my barley-sugar, Ettie'. 'Hush, children, this is something you will be able to put into your reminiscences' (Governess).

Anyhow I laughed aloud at 'By order of the Czar', though there were tears in my eyes too.

> The B.B.C. has many a ranter,
> And oft its programme interest lacks:
> But ah, for me there's one enchanter –
> Too seldom heard. His name is Max.

All that I can offer you in return, at present, is a laboriously composed 'middle' which I wrote for the *Spectator*, by request, on *The Dynasts* in Wartime. (It will appear this week.) My journalistic output during the War has been limited to four items.

(i) Centenary article on T. Hardy for *John o'London's Weekly* [7 June 1940]

(ii) Review of T. Hardy's *Selected Poems* for the *Spectator* [6 September 1941]

(iii) Article on Aliveness in Literature for the *Fortnightly*, in which I somehow didn't mention Hardy – or did I? – I forget!

(iv) The above-mentioned item [6 February 1942]

Some day, perhaps, I may emerge from Max Gate and do a rattling good article on Parson Woodforde, which would indeed create a sensation in Fleet Street!

After failing to finish my prose book last April I gave it seven months' rest, and am now struggling with the last three chapters.

---

[1] 'Music Halls of My Youth', broadcast on 18 January 1942, in which Max sang some of the old songs.

I have corrected the galley-proofs of the first nine chapters, so I hope to send you some page-proofs in a few weeks' time. You will probably find it rather a relief to be reading a book about 'practically nothing happening' in 1909–1914. One's daily reading of the world's news is so consistently violent that one really does long for a day when nothing has happened. 'Nightingale Heard in Surrey'. What a headline that would be!

Or even this – from *The Times* 14 February 1939

SNOOKER

THE PROFESSIONAL
CHAMPIONSHIP

FROM OUR BILLIARDS CORRESPONDENT

Nevertheless I look forward to the time when Winston will once again be building a wall at his house near Westerham (or will he build a Blenheim?) though I fear that he will find life a little flat and uneventful when his invaluable efforts are at an end (*providential*, surely, as well as invaluable, for who else is there who could have led us along?)

There isn't much news from Heytesb'ry;
It's a quiet old spot, as you know.
Things jog along here somehow,
And what *we* call fast is *slow*.
Flowers bloom slow in the garden;
Birds pipe slow on the tree.
Everything goes on slowly;
But the slowest of all is ME!

(Chorus)   Captain Sassoon is a slow old chap
As he plods around the place.
'E's a kind old bloke, and he loves 'is joke,
But the biggest joke is 'is face!

With much love from us all to you and Florence.   S.S.

Dearest Max, 'At long last' I am able to send you my one and only page-proof of *The Weald of Youth*. I haven't been through it, but I revised the galleys very carefully, so hope that there is nothing much wrong. It is sad that we can't talk about it together. There are so many little points which I should have liked to discuss with you – especially about Gosse. (I tried to put him in only as I was capable of observing him at the time.) I don't like the idea of putting you to trouble in writing comments and suggestions, but if you notice anything in grammar or punctuation or inept epithet which needs altering, please pencil your queries. With love from us all to you and Florence.   S.S.

Dearest Max, Since the word 'everywhhere' on January 18,[1] I had not listened to one word on the wireless until last night, 'When once again I heard with mute acclaim The voice of Beerbohm, much respected name'. I hope you appreciate the compliment as much as I delighted in your delicious homily against vulgarity. (When you said 'on the Soap's behalf' both Hester and I 'laughed unaffectedly'. The word *behalf* – exquisitely funny.) But I mustn't butter you up too much or you will be getting above yourself – 'the idol of the radio public?' ... Well, there isn't much news from here except dull news. Like the non-milk-producing goat in our paddock, 'sometimes I sits and thinks, and sometimes I just sits'. Hester, on the other hand, scarcely sits down at all, what with running after George and doing the housework; for we have no servants except the cook and a volatile charwoman, who comes and goes when she listeth. I do indeed wash up and wipe a fair number of cups and plates, shut numerous shutters at blackout-time, and prepare George's vesperal cup of cocoa. My labours have lately been comforted by numerous nectarines, kindly allowed me by our

---

[1] Max's 'Advertisements', broadcast on 18 January, ended '*Good* night, children ... everywhhere'.

local wasps, who have been multitudinous this year. On my fifty-sixth birthday I was visited by two golden-crested wrens – migrants who vanished next day. Our only visitor in August was Sydney Cockerell.[1] July brought us Eddie Marsh, who spent most of his time weeding the flower-beds, but regaled us with many a pithy anecdote (unlike me, he demonstrates brevity being the soul of wit).

There was indeed one period of twenty-four hours, in August, when we had about forty visitors in the house, each one with a man-servant. This, however, was compulsory entertainment, the Guards Division were doing manoeuvres, and their Supply Column and Signals H.Q. were quartered here. The officers did themselves well in the dining-room, and the cook from Brooks's Club (I beg his pardon – chef) disported himself in the kitchen – not altogether satisfied with our frying-pans. I was recovering from flu, and had bad bronchitis, and it was pouring with rain; so I found the proceedings rather trying. At the present moment my only visitor is a very small field-mouse, which boldly explores my carpet in quest of wheat-grains – my evening occupation lately having been rubbing and sifting wheat-ears, which I collect in my capacious pockets while out riding; and shall distribute among our hard-eyed fowls, though a good deal of the grain will go to the much more charming chaffinches who visit my window-ledges in winter. I haven't been to London – or anywhere else – since December. I cut my own hair, which doesn't seem to look as bad as one would expect. I also cut all the thistles in the park, in the vain hope that they won't come up again next year. I have a feeling that I shall end my life as a professional mole-catcher (employed by the State when Heytesbury House has been made into a rest-home for decayed journalists). But who – even H.G. – can say what the future holds in store for us?... I don't suppose the politicians know any more about it than the moles, who have the merit of holding their tongues and doing their burrowing capably. But I wax sarcastic. What a social satirist I am!

Soon I shall be mailing you a presentably attired copy of *The*

---

[1] 1867–1962. Director of the Fitzwilliam Museum, Cambridge 1908–37. Knighted 1934.

Weald of Youth, for which I intend to design a bookplate. With love from us all to Florence and your dear self   S.S.

6 December 1942   *Heytesbury*

Dearest Max, I found this sheet of 1898 news at the back of a picture-frame today, and have read it since dinner with an agreeable sense of transportation to a quieter world. Can it be possible that the sensational *Daily Mail* of '98 was written in the style of an unsophisticated 'local paper' of 1942? O that we might revert to such journalism – is what I feel!

My book is reprinting (the first edition was 10,000). I suppose that in 1898 only Marie Corelli could achieve such sales – what a vulgarly successful autobiographer I am.

Yours ever   S.S.

The Rede Lecture: 1943[1]
Lytton, there's a Lecture – lustrous in Academe –
Yearly endowed for Cantabs by one *Rede*.
Thither on this day, with ears agog to heed,
Thronged the begowned ... Guess what was chosen as theme
Of the discourse which someone must deliver?
'Not *Me*?' you pipe. (Methinks I feel you shiver.)

---

[1] On Lytton Strachey, delivered by Max in the Senate House at Cambridge on 20 May 1943 and published as a pamphlet on 25 June.

Strachey, your supposition proves correct.
The subject of the Lecture was your Writings.
'Ruthlessly reconsidered!' you suspect,
'And disestablished by censorious slightings.'

Cheer up, old bean. Be radiant and rejoice.
Heaven succoured you from criticaster quacks.
Eminently late-Victorian was the voice;
Your Eulogist – our friend 'Mellifluous Max'.

20 May 1943

3 August 1943   *Heytesbury*

Dearest Non-Epistolary Max, It must have been more than two
months ago that I sent you some lines about the Rede Lecture, so
I will follow them up; and indeed it is high time that I thanked
you for the delight your lecture gave me.

I bought it at Hatchard's on June 30, within an hour of my
arrival in London, for my first visit to the capital since the end of
1941. Lecture in hand, I was walking along Charing Cross Road
soon afterwards, and by an odd chance passed Mr Schiff, who
was looking very like your portrait of 'Stephen Hudson'. (This
afternoon I amused myself by making a copy of the head of your
'Queen Victoria' Lytton, which I have stuck in my copy of 'the
Rede'.) On June 30, you may be amused to hear, I dined with
Lady Cholmondeley,[1] whose invitation had caused my visit to
London (and it was an invitation delivered with grace and *firmness*).
The fact was that Wavell had expressed a wish to meet me (just
fancy that!) as he is an enthusiast about poetry. Desmond was
there, and I spent a perfect evening, in surroundings which I can
only describe as palatial (Kensington Palace Gardens). Lady C, in
white satin, was charming, and I quite 'fell for her', though the
tempo of my conversational form felt a bit too like Handel's Largo –
no humming-bird talker I. (Lady C, like Philip, does dart from
flower to flower, sipping the nectar, and even Desmond couldn't
get quite enough latitude for discourse.) Wavell is very nice. No

---

[1] Sister of Sir Philip Sassoon and wife of the fifth Marquess of Cholmondeley.

small talk; a typical honest, intelligent Colonel (retired list). He has sent me his anthology of poetry, which is to be published in the autumn;[1] and Ivor Brown[2] has asked me to review it for the *Observer*. Which seems to be all the prose I am likely to write until liberated from being an 'odd-man' and dish-washer.

Existence here has been rather a struggle against domestic difficulties. During June we were altogether without servants – not so much as a charwoman set foot in our premises. Hester cooked gallantly, and I did a variety of things (and so did George, but *his* things weren't constructive) and it was extremely wearing. Now we are in clover, as G's old nannie has come to the rescue and does the cooking, and a couple of women from the village are lending a hand. I have bought a Jersey cow, and my main occupation is that of a dairymaid. Skimming cream is rather soothing, and turning the handle of the churn produces a pleasant vacuity of mind.

On November 1 we are expecting eight American officers and twelve servants; there is to be a General, and the fifteen London children and their matron must make way for this party. None of the rooms we use will be requisitioned, and the War Office is presenting us with a new hot-water boiler! The Colonel who came to arrange about it assured me that the War will be over by November! And really it does seem just possible that he is right.

In June I got a very nice little pony for George, and we go for rides together. He bumps along cheerfully, and makes a sweet picture – pure Caldecott.[3] We have had no visitors all the summer, except a man named Seago, who is a camouflage officer at Salisbury.[4] He is very lively and amusing, and quite a good painter – a disciple of Arnesby Brown,[5] and has just published a very charming book illustrated with some of his pictures.[6] The lawn is unmown, and prettily adorned by harebells; otherwise Heytesbury

---

[1] *Other Men's Flowers* (1944), compiled by Field-Marshal Lord Wavell. The *Observer* review was written by George Orwell.

[2] Author and journalist (1891–1974). Editor of the *Observer* 1942–8.

[3] Randolph Caldecott (1846–86), chiefly known as illustrator of children's books.

[4] Edward Seago, painter and author (1910–72).

[5] Painter (1866–1955). Knighted 1938.

[6] *Peace in War* (1943).

is looking as usual – lovelier than ever, on the whole. With love from your loquacious old crony   S.S.

9 December 1945   *Heytesbury*

Dearest Max, Faber's are posting you my book,[1] and this letter must serve as inscription. And you know that I am your ever devoted adorer, and your debtor for innumerable hours of life made gracious and delightful (apart from what you give by your works). I am at present in rather a vortex of domestic upheavals, and feeling – like most of us – a profound fatigue after the war years and their exactions. So will be brief – only adding that I am much consoled by having acquired Henry James and Archbishop Benson, and 'The Jolly Corner'.[2] I ache to see you again; and *must* set about contriving it soon.

With much love to you and dear Florence from   S.S.

My pen thrills while writing your address on the envelope,[3] for I am more of a Meredithian than ever – about his poetry and the great passages of his prose.

26 August 1947   *Heytesbury*

Dearest Max, I have waited to hear, from my emissary, that my tribute was safely delivered. It occurred to me that, although a host of telegrams from Maximilians could not fail to gratify you, a slight shower of sherry and a drop or two of your favourite maraschino might add variety to the celebrations.[4] Can sherry convey affection? Mine tried to ... The pleasant and providential Karn now writes that he found you in your usual adorable form. With a sigh, I wish it had been me who found you. About a year ago someone – I forget who – informed me that you and Florence had returned to Rapallo, and I bowed to the inevitable. Last week

---

[1] *Siegfried's Journey*, published on 7 December 1945.
[2] Two of Max's caricatures.
[3] Flint Cottage, Box Hill, Dorking, George Meredith's old home, where the Beerbohms were staying.
[4] In 1942, to honour Max's seventieth birthday, a number of distinguished and devoted admirers founded the Maximilian Society, which every year sent him large quantities of wine as birthday presents.

a little bird sent me your real address, and I rejoice that you are in Ellis Roberts's house. Has he left you his cassock, and do you deputise for him at Sunday evening services?[1]

Well, Max, I have completed my biography of Meredith, a task which I undertook with much anxiety and effected with enormous drudgery last winter. Could you have predicted such a thing? I couldn't. 'Mercutio between four-wheeler shafts', was Mrs Cryptic-Sparkler's phrase for it.[2] Let it stand at that. Meredithians will find my comments elementary. But Trevelyan[3] countenanced the proceedings with preliminary encouragement, and I have illustrated adequately with copious quotations from contemporary critics. O that I could have discussed my problems with you on Villino roof! What illumination there would have been for my intellectual opacities! Reading his novels, I found the style fatiguing for long stretches. But – as Henry James said to Desmond – 'he did the best things best'. And his best poems are indestructible.

Some time soon I shall be sending you my own *Collected Poems*, which Faber's despatched to the binders about three months ago. (Quite a tolerable green buckram.) When are yours coming out? Now that I am clear of G.M. I am hoping to write a few more; but my muse doesn't seem to approve of the present Government and the conditions under which we exist. I haven't been to London for fourteen months, but my rather monotonous months are enlivened by bouts of George, who keeps me busy and is an ideal companion, so quick-minded and affectionate and utterly rewarding in his attachment to me. It is perfect happiness. And, his prep-school being only three miles from here, I never lose sight of him for long. In September 1950 he will go on to Oundle (good for science and engineering, which is his obvious bent). But I try not to think of Oundle. It will be a pill to be swallowed philosophically.

With much love to you and dear Florence from   S.S.

---

[1] Roberts was a devout Anglo-Catholic with a gentle clerical manner.

[2] In 'Euphemia Clashthought', Max's parody of Meredith in *A Christmas Garland*, two such pithy sayings of Mrs Cryptic-Sparkler are reported, but this very Meredithian one seems to have been concocted by S.S.

[3] G.M. Trevelyan, the historian (1876–1962), to whom S.S. dedicated his *Meredith*, had published in 1906 *The Poetry and Philosophy of George Meredith*.

11 September [*1947*]   AS FROM *Highcroft, Edge,*
                                                    near Stroud, Glos.

Dearest of all Siegfrieds, How munificent and magnificent of you, and how like *you*, to send me such a gift! But how wrong of you! For I had asked Alan Dent[1] to impress on every one that nothing this time was to be given me, except some message of good will. You, however, proceeded to play the rogue elephant – charging up the Cotswolds and causing panic among the simple villagers of Edge, who had never seen any such spectacle. Dear friend, a thousand thanks and remonstrances. The sherry is very lovely – *and* the maraschino.

You know how bad I am at letter-writing, and I wish this letter could be expressive of what I feel – after all the time that has elapsed since last I wrote. How lovely your work has been meanwhile! Your revocations of your old self, and of all those scenes that you have passed through, and of all those men and women whom you have known – how magical in their skill, their delicacy, their warmth and depth! And now 'Mr Meredith's coach stops the way' – and Siegfried postpones himself, but not, I hope, for long? I shall look to you for guidance about him. He had been *the* idol of my youth. But in recent years, taking up one or other of his novels, I have been (though I hardly admitted to myself that I was) disappointed. About his greatness as a poet I feel sure that you are right. I shall try to love his poetry – though I fear it is too closely packed with philosophy for my weak head. I am in some ways a gifted person, but in sheer *brain-power* I have always been defective – or rather never above the average. Intuitions and fancies have been my line, and now, *aetat* seventy-five, I'm not very good even at them.

I write from Duke's Hotel in London. I am going to Ireland for a couple of days, to see my dear sister Agnes, who now lives there. And then, on the 23rd of this month Florence and I start back for Italy. We shall be in London two days before that. Is there any chance of your being in London at that time? Florence, who loves you as much as I do, does hope there may be some such chance. Please give my love to George, and Florence's. Your devoted

                                                                    MAX

---

[1] Author, critic and journalist (1905–78), organiser of the Maximilians.

What a charming fellow Mr Glass is![1] I wonder if you would tell me his Christian name and his address. For I want to thank him for a note that he wrote to me the day after his visit, and I could not find his note afterwards.

14 September 1947   *Heytesbury*

Dearest Max, Your lovely letter is a great comfort to me. But I must restrain my pen, as you are in a vortex of departure, and your 'trip to Ireland' must have been an exacting – though rewarding – effort. Alas, I cannot be in London next week-end, as I must be here looking after George, and cannot leave him alone. He is returning on Tuesday from Mull,[2] where he has been having a splendid time and reviving his vitality with good air and food. I have been completely alone for the last six weeks, and have found the time difficult to get through.

Circumstances – and my tendency to stay where I am – have somehow kept me here for more than a year: in fact I've only had one meal away from this house since 1 September 1946! And the conditions of life seem to make it impossible for my few remaining friends to come and see me here. My one gain has been that I've managed to get the Meredith book finished – 95,000 words of it! – and old Mr Kyllmann, the head director of Constable's who knew G.M. fairly well for the last fourteen years of his life, says that it exceeds his expectations and gives a fully satisfactory picture of G.M.

Cyril Karn's address is 7 Lansdown Place, Cheltenham. (How right of you to call him 'Mr Glass'!) I am utterly unrepentant about the sherry. Had it been possible, I would have sent you a ton of caviar and all the pearls of Ethiopia. Could – oh could – dear Florence send me just a few lines in two or three months' time – to say that you are both finding things reasonably easy at the Villino? It would be a relief to my mind. You will be so much in my thoughts.

---

[1] Max's name for Cyril Karn.
[2] Where Hester was now living.

I have had a peck of worry in the last three-and-a-half years, and the thought of my valued friends is a needed sustenance. But I am resolved to see it through, for George's sake; and for the task of giving him guidance I continue to exist. Otherwise I might feel that the world has been too much for me (as most of us do nowadays). And, like you, I am not tough and prefer civilisation to barbarity. Anyhow, I hope that you will feel that my *Collected Poems* are a tolerable contribution to decent values. As a sequence they show, I think, a steady development, from the infantile to the grown-up. And now, dearest Max, bless you – ever and always.

S.S.

28 June 1948   *Heytesbury*

Dearest Max, Tomorrow a young man is coming here to see me. He has been made known to me by a friend as about to visit Rapallo. All I know of him, so far, is that he is at Oxford, draws wittily for *Punch*, and writes quite good unmodern verse.[1] He is, of course, hungry to meet you. So I am utilising him as my postman, and he will hand to you this proof-copy of my *Meredith*, which – with old-ladylike timidity – I was afraid to send by ordinary post, doubting whether it would reach you! Would that I could talk it over with you. But all I can do is to hope that you will find it 'good reading'. It is, of course, only an *outline* of his life and work. What else *could* it be, when one knows so little of him as a living reality, and one's mental capacity for ideas is so limited compared with his? *Was* he, as Gosse wrote in one of his last letters, 'essentially unreal in his work and character'? I prefer to think otherwise.

Since your departure I have jogged along as usual here – only away once, in April, for ten days, when I took George to the Norfolk Broads and had a lovely time. I haven't felt able to tackle any more prose-writing yet, but must attempt it next winter, I suppose, merely for occupation in the evenings. But I begin to dread the fatigue of it. It doesn't seem natural to me to drudge out

---

[1] Haro Hodson, artist (born 1923).

tens of thousand of words at a stretch for Messrs Faber! I long to be limited and exquisite – on large paper, in limp vellum with green silk ties!

Meanwhile T.S.E. has been elevated to utmost eminence – among us authors (surely a sign of the times we live in?). The younger generation compares him with Milton. I suppose he *is* very important, for this age. But will Posterity find much in his achievement? What *has* he said that will ring on for their ears? It really puzzles me. And I assume that you also regarded the announcement of his O.M. with dissatisfaction.

During the past week I have been busily occupied, sorting out and stowing away most of the contents of Weirleigh, which arrived in two huge vans.[1] What memories many of the things evoked! Things I've known ever since I can remember – old candlesticks which remind me of 'going up to bed' in the Nineties – old clocks which ticked away my days of childhood (fragrant nostalgia touch). Well, Max, all I can say in conclusion is that I wish I could get into young Mr Haro Hodson's skin and be with you on the Villino roof for an afternoon. But I have my ever precious memories, and for them I thank whatever gods there be. With much love to you and Florence   S.S.

P.S. The young man has spent an evening with me, and I feel sure you will like him.

[Postcard with picture of Torosay Castle, Isle of Mull]

[Late August 1948][2]   [*Mull*]

Dearest Max and Florence, It seems that Haro is my deputy-describer of holiday life in Mull, so I will merely leave it to him, and say how much I have enjoyed hearing his Villino Chiaro news.

Mull is lovely and poetic scenery; but it has rained nearly every day, and I begin to wish for the library at Heytesbury, whither we return on September 16th (the day of *Meredith* publication).

With much love from S.S.

---

[1] S.S.'s mother had died on 11 July 1947, aged ninety-three.
[2] S.S. reached Mull on 21 August.

Dearest Max, I might have written to you before, but was ill with influenza – and could find no words to send you. But my thoughts have been with you often, in sadness for your loss; and you know how I loved dear Florence and I appreciated her wonderful qualities.[1] You know it all, and how I treasure the lovely hours we have had together – flawless felicity and memories of delighted companionship with you both. I have prayed that you might be sustained by your philosophic mind – and that is all I can say – except that I keep on saying to myself 'Who is going to look after beloved Max?'

And now I must tell you, hoping it may amuse you, that I attended the Investiture this morning, and was duly C.B.E.'d by His Majesty, who gave me a charming smile, said he was glad to see me, and hoped that I was as busy as ever. (Well, Mr Gibbon, 'still scribbling, scribbling, scribbling?') It was touching and impressive, to watch the kindly way in which he patiently hooked all those O.B.E.s and M.B.E.s on to their humble recipients. What a good, modest man he is! The gentleman behind me, with whom I sat and conversed afterwards, was the head of the Crown Derby China manufactory – a very nice old boy, with whom I got on pleasantly.

So that was that; and I emerged into the Mall feeling rather cheered up by it all. I came out of the Throne Room behind the six Beefeaters, so was able to have a good look at their charming clothes and rosetted shoes. One of them was wearing pince-nez, and they all looked very gentle and mild and silver-haired. Lord Clarendon has a peculiar face, with an odd chin-beard. He looked rather seventeenth-century, I thought. While I was about to step up to the King, I was – nervously – able to be aware that the band in the gallery was playing 'I'll see *you* again, whenever spring breaks through again',[2] and suppressed a smile, as the eye of a very stern-looking Admiral was upon me, standing there to signal me onward to the presence. Anyhow, I was the only literary man there (Desmond having been knighted the week before) and the arts

---

[1] Florence Beerbohm died in early January 1951.
[2] From Noel Coward's *Bitter Sweet*.

were otherwise represented only by a film director named Wilcox,[1] who looked as if he were just going to be married, except that he'd omitted the white spats.

I absorbed every comma of your George Moore with enchantment, as I did your heavenly Tree and Hall Caine.[2] When I hear your voice it brings tears to my eyes. And why not? It is a voice from the Paradise of my happy past. And my heart is always yours, dear Max.   With love from S.S.

George won a scholarship at Oundle last June, and is very happy there. He is the greatest comfort to me, so lively and intelligent; he has become a keen biologist, and evidently takes after his uncle Oliver.[3]

24 August 1952   *Heytesbury*

Dearest Max, I could write reams of congratulation;[4] but you are inundated; so I have restricted myself to an innocent tribute which can take its modest place on your mantelpiece. And some time, when the echoes of ovation have subsided, I will send you such news as can emerge from my secluded existence. You will be pleased to hear that George and his quick-working brain are doing very well at Oundle. They say that he ought to win a major scholarship at King's, Cambridge, in science. He is also a vigorous and amusing prose-writer. Your ever grateful and affectionate

S.S.

---

[1] Herbert Wilcox (1890–1977). Husband of Dame Anna Neagle.
[2] Two of Max's broadcasts, 'George Moore' on 6 October 1950, and 'Nat Goodwin – and Another' on 30 May 1949.
[3] Hester's brother, Oliver Gatty.
[4] On his eightieth birthday.

A TRIBUTE TO SIR MAX BEERBOHM
by Siegfried Sassoon[1]

Most of us have a hazy idea of what Elysium ought to be like. But the majority, I presume, picture it as an abode they have never yet visited, and its circumstantial elements elude them. My one Elysium would unmistakably be established at Rapallo. I should be with Max, on the roof of the Villino Chiaro. It would be an afternoon of early summer, and Time would run back and fetch the age of gold, as Milton remarked.[2] Many and many an hour have I spent in that actual Elysium, sitting, or sauntering to and fro with him, while the blue Mediterranean looked its best and the coast highway below was not yet become bedevilled by the din of traffic which he, in old age, so philosophically endured – a road on which, as he said, a motor-car could once create excitement, and on which little children ran races during a great part of the day.

It was there – getting on for thirty years ago – that I began to know him well, though he had occasionally encountered my immature self since 1916, when I was introduced to him by Edmund Gosse.

It was there that I experienced – more absolutely, I believe, than elsewhere – the art of comporting an exquisitely civilised conversation. Fortunate were those who likewise enjoyed that felicity. They will agree that Elysian was the only word for what he gave us. And dear Florence Beerbohm was there as universal provider of angelic hospitality.

What *was* the keyword to this atmosphere of charmed composure which he created? *Leisurely*. Just that. His friend Desmond Mac-Carthy has described how, when a young man, 'his walk was slow and tranquil, such as one could hardly imagine ever breaking into a run'. For myself I can record that I never saw him make a hurried movement. All his proceedings were controlled and deliberate. He

---

[1] Max died on 20 May 1956. This tribute was recorded at Heytesbury on 28 June and broadcast, produced by Douglas Cleverdon, on 22 August.
[2] In his 'Hymn on the Morning of Christ's Nativity'.

went his ways with the unhastening deportment of a swan – though not, of course, with a swan's proud insulted look.

More than once I have watched him do an extempore drawing to illustrate something we had been discussing. The purposeful pencil took its own time: and like his conversational style, the hand's behaviour was deft, serene, and self-diverting. His attitude to existence was a courteous tolerance of the raucous uproar of human affairs, and an undeviating private formula of beautiful manners. After hearing one of his wartime broadcasts, I wrote to him, in a delirium of gratitude and escape from black-out beastliness, that it was as though I had been listening to the voice of the last civilised man on earth. On which he probably commented – as he afterwards did about another of my enthusiasms – 'What utter bosh! But – what delightful bosh!' Disclaim my encomium though he might, he remained in conspicuous contrast to that decline of the graces which he had, long since, observed and deplored.

In his early essays he had posed himself somewhat as the fastidious trifler. Beau Beerbohm was the public figure he chose to adopt – and what attitude else, one wonders, could have conformed to his artistic perfectionism? But let me warn the uninitiated – and how I envy them their initiation – against believing that his was the artificial euphuism of a dandified dilettante. For behind that studied elegance, that insistence on scrupulous refinement of utterance, was the toughest of professional experts – the brilliant and formidable dramatic critic, the sprightly but uncompromising caricaturist, the superfine story-teller, and the cumulatively accomplished essayist, who was also an unassuming but percipient moralist.

Unassuming he indeed was. 'My gifts are small,' he once remarked to me, 'but I've used them discreetly, never exceeding my limitations. My range is extremely restricted. It reaches to Knightsbridge – certainly not as far as West Kensington.' It is true that, over and over again, he called himself a *petit maître*. 'I love best in literature,' he avowed, 'delicate and elaborate ingenuities of form and style.'

Can any superb master-craftsman be classified as *petit maître*? I, for one, refuse to believe it. But I am not here to talk knowingly about his collected writings. I adore them all, and can only advise 'Read the lot, and good luck to you!'

I am here, however, to be unblushingly personal, and to luxuriate – for your enlightenment, I hope – in memories of the enrichments he bestowed on my mind. There was one episode which exemplified his great generosity to writers of a younger generation. In the spring of 1938 I went to Rapallo with the uncorrected page-proofs of my book *The Old Century*. Not many verbal alterations were needed. But I was aware of my punctuation being amateurishly unsystematic. And for Max punctuation was of prime importance to perfected prose. His own has an individuality inseparable from his sensitive manipulation of vocal cadences. Anyhow, he took mine firmly in hand, and went through every sentence of the book with me, consuming countless cigarettes, and conferring on me one of the most delectable and rewarding experiences of my career as an author. The volume was dedicated to him; and when sending him his copy I inscribed in it the following lines.

> Ah, what avails enormous sales!
> Ah, what unstinted praise!
> This book, with proud remembrance, hails
> Page-proof Rapallo days.
>
> Max, punctuation's pioneer
> The unbound *Old Century* through,
> Its every thought and cadence here
> I dedicate to you.[1]

With that little divulgement of artless homage he would, probably, prefer me to bid you good-bye. 'Make much of me in memory if you must,' he might mildly protest, 'but bear in mind that I am already a copiously reported character. There is nothing unfamiliar that you could profitably disclose. And, like the lady in Leonardo's picture, my "eyelids are a little weary"[2] – of those epithets,

---

[1] An echo of Landor's poem 'Rose Aylmer'.

[2] Walter Pater on Leonardo da Vinci's Gioconda in his *Studies in the History of the Renaissance* (1873).

perennially applied to me, incomparable, and inimitable.' Tell them, he might advise me, if it improves your performance, that we played parlour games together; that I walked in your woodland inhaling the scent of syringa; that you beheld me in a double-breasted, quilted, purple silk smoking-jacket of the Edwardian Era; and that I make it a rule, always to lie down for an hour after luncheon. But avoid undue ventriloquism, while dandling my post-terrestrial presence so indulgently. And so obedient to his ventriloquised command, I brace myself to become, awhile, prudently impersonal.

There is a drawing, dated 1923, in which he represents himself – spectacled, skull-capped, and long-white-bearded – seated at his desk executing a caricature. Before him stand three rising young caricaturists, Lynch, Kapp, and 'Quiz', to be exact.[1] In the sky above the Portofino headland and the bay of Rapallo his tiny handwriting notes that they are 'wondering how long the veteran exile will go doddering on'. Needless to say, this bit of badinage had no sting in it. All three were his devoted admirers. For the next nine years or so the 'veteran exile' continued to entertain us with ironic recordings of the contemporary scene. And then, as I have heard him say, the impulse toward caricature forsook him. He had, he thought, somehow mislaid his sense of disrespect. For a time, it seemed that we were in danger of hearing little more from him. His body had never been robust, and the nervous output of prolonged literary composition had become daunting to him. But one evening in the last week of 1935 an unpredictable event occurred.

Dulcet, demure, impeccably managed and modulated, a voice was overheard 'on the air' – the voice of Max. He was revisiting the London of his childhood and youth, when Hampstead and Chelsea were villages, and Mayfair, St James's, and Westminster still places of leisure. Having outlived some of that London's individuality and charm, he pronounced a politely acrimonious *cri-de-coeur* against the thing it had become – democratised, commercialised, mechanised, standardised, vulgarised, and, above all,

---

[1] Bohun Lynch (1884–1928), Edmond X. Kapp (1890–1978) and Powys Evans (1899–1982).

victimised by extensive havoc wrought upon its architectural beauties. It was a forthright manifesto against modernism. But it won the great heart of that public which he had hitherto so fastidiously avoided. A heaven-born broadcaster had arrived.

It was in the summer of 1936 that I enjoyed for the first time the privilege of being, so to speak, entertained by him in my own house. For more than a week the vintage quality of his company kept me in a condition of Maximilian inebriation. He was at his liveliest, and gave us full measure of his delicious impersonations. His imitations of King Edward VII reduced me to helpless hilarity, and I was specially attached to an aristocratic Major who was in the habit of announcing, '*My* mother, who was a *very* great lady'. When enacting the Major, his face seemed to change and become an epitome of a conventional clubman, rotund, exclusive, and a shade overbearing toward social inferiors.

During these idyllic days he happened to be preparing his broadcast *A Small Boy Seeing Giants*, and the murmur of his voice was often heard from the bedroom where he was perfecting the delivery of this masterpiece of affectionate retrospection.

The Giants he was to evoke so graphically were the Victorian statesmen of the 1880s. I chanced to have in my library an 1876 collection of 'Spy' cartoons of politicians and 'Men of the Day' extracted from *Vanity Fair*. Though unaware of its pertinence to his discourse, one rainy afternoon I cunningly produced the album and sat with him for a memorable half-hour while he turned the pages with delicate deliberation, entrancing me with reminiscent responses to their period appeal, and concluding with some incisive comments on the present-day extinction of singularity in male attire.

It pleases me to imagine that his nostalgic inspection of my album had some remote kinship with the ensuing passage from the then undelivered broadcast, in which you will hear once more his incomparable vocal cadence:

I am what the writers of obituary notices call 'an interesting link with the past'. I wish I could have foreseen the future. Had I done so – had I known how exactly, how furtively like one another our rulers would try to look – I should have revelled even more than I did revel at the sight of those men of 1884. Visually, they let themselves go, without self-consciousness or fear. Each one of them was a law unto himself. Some of them – Lord Kimberley, for example, and Mr Dodson – had beards without moustaches. Some of them were clean-shaven. One of them, Mr Shaw-Lefevre, had always what looked like a four days' growth of beard. Lord Hartington's beard and moustache were far longer than Sir Charles Dilke's. Mr Joseph Chamberlain was content with small side-whiskers. Sir William Harcourt had a 'Newgate frill'. So had Lord Northbrook, who wore, however and moreover, a becoming tuft on the chin. The wide, pale, pleasantly roguish face of old Lord Granville was framed in masses of silvery curls. Some wore their hair long, others short. Some of them dressed badly, others – in an off-hand way – well. To none of them except Chamberlain and Dilke, those two harbingers of another age, would one have applied the epithet *neat*. Believe me, they offered no end of latitude to the limner.

And may I add that he himself has provided no end of latitude to an appreciative posterity. *Max Vobiscum.*

Index